August von Kotzebue

Pizarro - The Spaniards in Peru

The death of Rolla. A tragedy, in five acts - the original of the play

performing at the Theatre Royal Drury-Lane, under the title of Pizarro

August von Kotzebue

Pizarro - The Spaniards in Peru
The death of Rolla. A tragedy, in five acts - the original of the play performing at the
Theatre Royal Drury-Lane, under the title of Pizarro

ISBN/EAN: 9783337383022

Printed in Europe, USA, Canada, Australia, Japan

Cover: Foto ©Andreas Hilbeck / pixelio.de

More available books at **www.hansebooks.com**

PIZARRO.

THE
SPANIARDS IN PERU;
OR, THE
DEATH OF ROLLA.
A TRAGEDY,
IN FIVE ACTS:
BY AUGUSTUS VON KOTZEBUE.

THE ORIGINAL OF THE PLAY PERFORMING

AT THE

THEATRE ROYAL DRURY LANE,

UNDER THE TITLE OF

Pizarro.

TRANSLATED FROM THE GERMAN

BY ANNE PLUMPTRE;

TRANSLATOR OF KOTZEBUE'S VIRGIN OF THE SUN, &c,

Fourth Edition, revised.

LONDON:

PRINTED FOR R. PHILLIPS, NO. 71, ST. PAUL'S
CHURCH-YARD.

SOLD BY H. D. SYMONDS, AND T. HURST, PATERNOSTER-ROW;
CARPENTER AND CO. OLD BOND-STREET, R. H. WESTLEY,
STRAND; AND BY ALL OTHER BOOKSELLERS.

[*Price Half-a-Crown.*]

1799.

THE

AUTHOR's PREFACE.

———

THIS Drama is a continuation of my VIR-
GIN OF THE SUN. At the fuggeftion of my
friend Schrœder, many trifling alterations have
been made from the original manufcript.
Thefe, from refpect for his modefty, I might
have been difpofed to pafs over in filence, did
not more powerful reafons urge their being
pointed out. In the firft place, the opinion of fo
excellent a dramatic critic as Schrœder, muft
always be confidered as of great weight, and as
giving a fanction to whatever has paffed fuch an
ordeal: And fecondly, did I not explain how
far I am indebted to him, the applaufe which
the Piece has obtained, might excite the envious
and malicious to infinuate, that even a greater
fhare of that applaufe is due to my friend than
the reality would juftify. Some of the alterations were actually made by Schrœder himfelf,

others

others were undertaken by me, from hints which
he furnished.

Among the former, the principal were the
suppreſſion of the ſcene where Diego is brought
as a priſoner into the Spaniſh camp, which in
Schrœder's opinion interrupted the general effect
of the Firſt Act by a piece of mirth, unſeaſonably
introduced, as having no neceſſary connection
with the reſt of the Play ;*—alſo the omiſſion of
a Chorus, and an Air ſung by Elvira to the
guitar; and, above all, the removal of one very
dark ſhade from Pizarro's character, who, in the
original endeavours, in violation of his word ſolemnly given, to get Rolla again into his power.
The laſt and moſt advantageous of Schrœder's
own alterations, is making Pizarro gueſs at Elvira's deſign upon his life, which originally was
diſcovered to him by Rolla in very harſh terms ;
a circumſtance undoubtedly detracting, in ſome
meaſure, from the general grandeur of Rolla's
character.

* By a miſtake of the Printer's, this ſcene is retained in the
publication. *Note by the Author.*

The Tranſlator has alſo retained it, as not entering into the
force of Schrœder's objection.

Among my own alterations, made at the fuggeftion of Schrœder, may be noticed the change
of Valverde from Pizarro's chaplain to his fecre-
trary. To this I was induced from a conviction,
that it muft invariably excite difguft, to behold,
either upon the great theatre of the world itfelf,
or the little theatre, which is only an epitome of
the greater, a clergyman of fo contemptible a
character. It was indeed my intention that this
alteration fhould have been confined to the
Stage ; and that in the clofet the Prieft, who
is no fictitious perfonage, fhould appear in his
native unworthinefs : yet at laft I had neither
time nor inclination to trouble myfelf farther
about fuch a wretch ; and I therefore let him
remain as he now ftands.

But the moft important change the Piece has
undergone, and that for which I feel myfelf moft
deeply indebted to the fuggeftions of my friend,
is the elevation of mind now given to Elvira ; and
I truft that this character, which doubtlefs, in the
original, approached too nearly to that of a common proftitute, will in its prefent form excite both
compaffion and admiration.

Some

Some other alterations propofed by Schrœder, I declined to adopt, fince they appeared dictated by no other principle than a miftaken compliance with the times. As for inftance, the omiffion of that paffage where I notice the Papal Bulls, by one of which America was granted to the Spaniards, and by the other the Indians were determined to be *Men*, not *Apes*,—as well as that wherein I mention the Thirteen Indians who were hung in honour of Chrift and his Apoftles. Thefe are hiftorical facts, which I can fee no folid reafon againft introducing upon the Stage.*

* The Tranflator has omitted the remainder of the Preface; as it has no relation to the prefent work, but refers entirely to two other of the Author's Dramas, its infertion appeared fuperfluous.

Plays of Kotzebue's *published by the same Translator,* and to be had of all the Bookfellers,

THE NATURAL SON.
(LOVERS' VOWS)
SIXTH EDITION.

THE COUNT OF BURGUNDY.
SECOND EDITION.

THE FORCE OF CALUMNY.
SECOND EDITION.

THE VIRGIN OF THE SUN.
THIRD EDITION.
Each Price Half-a-Crown.

Published alfo by R. PHILLIPS,

SELF IMMOLATION,
Tranflated from KOTZEBUE, by Mr. NEUMAN;

AND

The CASTLE OF MONTVAL,
A TRAGEDY,
By the Rev. T. S. WHALLEY,
As performed at DRURY LANE.

DRAMATIS PERSONÆ.

ATALIBA, *King of Quito.*

ROLLA,
ALONZO DE MOLINA, } *Generals in the Peruvian Army.*

CORA, *Wife to Alonzo.*

PIZARRO, *General of the Spanish Army.*

ELVIRA, *his Mistress.*

ALMAGRO,
GONZALO,
DAVILA, } *Officers in the Spanish Army.*
GOMEZ,

VALVERDE, *Secretary to Pizarro.*

LAS-CASAS, *a Dominican Friar.*

DIEGO, *Attendant on Molina.*

An OLD CAZIQUE.

An OLD MAN.

A BOY.

A COURTIER.

SPANISH SOLDIERS, PERUVIAN SOLDIERS, PRIESTS,
COURTIERS, WOMEN, *and* CHILDREN.

THE

SPANIARDS IN PERU;

OR THE

DEATH OF ROLLA.

ACT I.

SCENE I.—*The inside of* PIZARRO's *Tent in the Spanish Camp.*

ELVIRA *in Man's Apparel, sleeping upon a Couch.* VALVERDE *enters softly, looks at her passionately for a few Moments, then kneels by her, and kisses her Hand as it hangs down.* ELVIRA *wakes, and casts upon him a Look of pointed Indignation.*

VALVERDE.

FORGIVE the effect of your charms.

Elvira. Oh wonderful!—that you should be likely to perform a miracle.

Valverde. A miracle!—What miracle?

Elvira. No less than to set a woman at variance with her own beauty.

Valverde. You are very severe.

Elvira. Why did you disturb my dreams?—they were so pleasing!

Valverde. Of what were you dreaming?

Elvira. That I saw you hanging.

B   *Valverde.*

Valverde. How long will Elvira revile my love?

Elvira. Your love!—Who would give fo honourable an appellation to a fentiment fo fpurious and bafe?—Between ourfelves, Valverde, when you talk of love, you refemble a beggar afking alms, and then fnatching the purfe from the hand that was about to relieve him, while at the fame time he invoked God's blefling upon the charity.

Valverde. What dare not a lovely woman fay?

Elvira. What dare not a coxcomb do?—Who gave you leave to come and difturb my fleep?—Is it not enough, that I am waked every night by the rattle of drums?—And yet I had rather that my ears were tormented, than my eyes.

Valverde. You are perfect miftrefs of the art of trying a man's patience.

Elvira. Would you wifh Pizarro to be informed of your proceedings?

Valverde. Rather tell me, by what fpell Pizarro holds you in fuch bondage? His eyes are wild and ftaring; his beard is fhaggy and uncombed;—he is a hypocrite in friendfhip, a tyrant in love.— —

Elvira. Hold!—this funeral fermon is premature!—remember he is not yet dead.

Valverde. Rough and unpolifhed, both in body and mind; a driver of fwine in his youth, he now rules men as if they were fwine.

Elvira. He fhews by this that he knows them accurately.

Valverde. Ignorant as an Andalufian mule-driver, this mighty hero cannot even read or write.

Elvira. My good friend, a woman devoted to love, concerns herfelf little whether the object of her paffion be learned or illiterate, for love is only written in the heart, and is to be read only in the eyes. Valour will much more eafily enchain the foul of a woman than learning. Pizarro fights with the fword, you with the pen—he fpills blood, you only fpill ink.

Valverde. I do not find that we have been hitherto much benefited by the effufion of either.

Elvira. Nor would all the ink ever contained by you, have enabled Nugnez Balboa to difcover the South Sea;

ftill lefs would ftudying the propofitions of Ariftotle have infpired Pizarro and Almagro with fpirit to fit out their frail veffel and encounter fo many dangers; but you might have remained groveling amid the duft of the fchools; while I had been immured in a convent.

Valverde. It yet remains a queftion, whether we are gainers or lofers by our prefent altered fituations.

Elvira. Monaftic uniformity! The flumber of a marmot! Heaven preferve me from fuch a life!

Valverde. This is always the cafe with women—they are never contented without eminence. Splendid mifery is more welcome to them, than calm repofe and domeftic happinefs.

Elvira. Do you know what is, above all things, their averfion? The intrufive babble of a preacher of common fayings.

Valverde. Scoff as you pleafe, madam, while the fun continues to fhine; but when the thunder rolls you may be awed;—and that moment is perhaps not far diftant.

Elvira. (*Scornfully*) Valverde turning prophet!— on what foundation may he build his dark oracles?

Valverde. Are we not in a foreign land, where death lies in ambufh for us, in every new plant, in every unknown fruit which hunger may impel us to tafte—and where thofe, whom the fword fpares, perifh from being unaccuftomed to the climate. Our numbers are daily diminifhing.

Elvira. Is not that a benefit to us?—fince the furvivors are their heirs.

Valverde. There is the point:—you are led away by your rapacity.

Elvira. And by what principle is Valverde led away? Do you fuppofe, that I cannot difcern the wolf becaufe he imitates the bleating of the fheep?—Do you imagine it poffible to veil the rogue from the eyes of a woman?— Away, away! believe me, that throughout the whole camp, not one perfon will be found who fpeaks his genuine fentiments,—Las-Cafas excepted.

Valverde. Name not that fanatic, with his vifions of humanity, and toleration.

B 2

Elvira.

Elvira. Name him not!—know, that there are moments, when the visions of this old man impress my heart so powerfully, that I could even kiss his grey beard; nor can I find any means of effacing the impression again, but by devoting the night to revelry.

Valverde. Shame on thee!

Elvira. Ah! had I but been blessed with an earlier knowledge of him; who can say what might have been my fate!

Valverde. A holy enthusiast in the cause of his beloved humanity, as it is pleased to style itself. And indeed nothing so easily leads men into enthusiasm, as a fine sounding word, which has no definite idea. The imagination groans, and the martyr is instantly born.

Elvira. Valverde a philosopher, too?

Valverde. Does that displease you?—Well, then, let us descend from the clouds of philosophy, to wander amid the flowers of love.

Elvira. They would wither beneath your footsteps. In short. groveler, if ever you hope to gain Elvira's love; you must throw away your pen, grasp a sword, and achieve some illustrious action.

Valverde. What mighty actions has Pizarro achieved?

Elvira. Ask both the old and the new world. By the force of his own talents, he has raised himself from the low station of a swine-driver, to the exalted rank of a warrior. When, in a small ship, and accompanied only by a hundred followers, he quitted Panama to conquer an unknown world; my heart whispered me, " *This must be a bold man.*" But, afterwards, when, in the little island of Gallo, he with his sword marked a line in the sand, and magnanimously desired those of his followers who were discontented, and wished to depart, to cross that line; when he was deserted by all but thirteen tried friends, who swore adherence to him at all hazards, at whose head he resolutely devoted himself to death, or the accomplishment of his purpose, my heart cried aloud, " *This is a great man!*"

Valverde. Great,—should he succeed; but, if his projects miscarry, the world will call him a fool.

Elvira

Elvira. The fate of every hero!—Children look with gaping mouths after a rocket that afcends boldly; but laugh, when one burfts in li_hting.

Valverde. But fhould this rocket rife till it reach the clouds, what would then b- your expectations?

Elvira. To become Vice-queen of Peru. Pizarro fhall govern this untutored peo: e; I will civilife them.

Valverde. Think you fo?—How little do you know Pizarro's crafty ambit n. Should fortune raife him to the height to which he afpires, his hand will doubt-lef· be offered to fome r.ch m: den, whofe high birth may caft a veil over the obfcurity of his own, and whofe con-nections at court may ferve as a fhield to protect him; while poor Elvira, with all that fhe has done and fuffered for his fake, will be inftantly forgotten.

Elvira. Ha.—fhould this be fo?—But, hifs on vene-mous reptile!

Valverde. And, on the contrary, fhould Pizarro's hum-ble fecretary b. promoted to the rank of his chancellor; Elvira m v i a fh 'er in Valverde's arms.

Elvir. Impude wretch!

Valverde. You trample down flowers which you might pluck, in aiming at fruit beyond your reach. Believe me, while Alonzo de Molina fhall continue to inftruct the Peruvians in our arts, Pizarro may be content to thrafh empty ftraw.

Elvira. And believe me, while I am convinced that Pizarro remains worthy of my affection, no petty ca'umn-ries fh. l effect our feparation. Should fortune turn her back upon him, if it be for no demerits of his own, Elvira will ftill take him by the hand.

Valverde. Repentance only hobbles on, it is true, yet it will at laft overtake fools.— Hift!—I hear his voice!

Elvira. Hafte, hypocrite!—and affume thy mafk of honour.

SCENE II.—*Enter* PIZARRO. *Seeing* ELVIRA *and* VAL-
VERDE *together, he ftarts, and obferves them both with an eye of dark fufpicion.* VALVERDE *bows obfequioufly.*
ELVIRA *laughs.*

Pizarro. Why do you laugh? *Elvira.*

Elvira. To laugh and weep we know not why,—is the privilege of woman.

Pizarro. But, I infift upon knowing your reafon.

Elvira. You may infift; but I fhall ftill be filent.

Valverde. Donna Elvira was ridiculing my fears.

Pizarro. What fears?

Valverde. Left the enemy through their fuperiority in numbers, and infpired by Alonzo——

Pizarro. Only a woman, and thofe who refemble women, could fear that boy.

Valverde. You are right; it was childifh pufillanimity. What arrogance and folly! He, a pupil of your's, trained under your ftandard, now dares to fet himfelf up in oppofition to his mafter!

Pizarro. He, who ate at my own table, who flept in my own tent.

Valverde. Ungrateful wretch!

Pizarro. He was entrufted by his mother to my care. She was a haughty woman; and I thought I difcovered in the breaft of this boy, a fpark of heroic fire which might eafily be fanned into a flame.

Elvira. 'Tis the province of our fex alone, to form heroes.

Pizarro. Do you think fo?—I have never loved.

Elvira. Then you cannot be a hero.

Pizarro. (*To Valverde*) Often as I have related to Alonzo the ftory of my firft expedition — how, with a handful of men, I was driven about for feventy days fucceffively — how ftorms and billows at fea, rivers, marfhes, and tracklefs forefts by land, made each ftep we took as toilfome as a day's journey — how, at one time, the wild inhabitants of the coaft, at another, the elements, combated againft us — how perpetual conflicts, hunger, a fultry climate, and fatal difeafes, daily diminifhed our little troop, till neceffity at laft compelled me to abandon a country curfed by the decrees of nature herfelf, and fave my life by feeking refuge on an inhofpitable fhore, oppofite to the Pearl Iflands.—Often, as I have defcanted on thefe things to Alonzo, has he, full of admiration, clafped me in his arms, while tears trembled in his fine blue eyes.

Valverde. And whofe feet trampled down this hopeful plant?   *Pizarro.*

Pizarro. Las-Cafas came with his fmooth tongue, and alked to him of moving in a higher fphere; till he intoxi-:ated him with enthufiafm; and from that hour I wearied nyfelf in vain, in endeavouring to draw my youthful charge 'rom his air-built caftles in the clouds, down to the real world below.

Valverde. Till, at length, he forfoo'; you, joined your enemies, and betrayed his native country.

Pizarro. But, firft, the boy was weak enough to at-tempt fhaking the principles of a man like Pizarro. He hung in tears about my neck, tried to wheedle the grafped fword out of my hand, called the Peruvians our bre-thren——

Valverde. Obftinate heathens our brethren!—there, indeed, I recognize Las-Cafas.

Pizarro. Finding, however, that his tears fell upon fenfelefs marble, he gave up the caufe, and went over to the enemy. Traitor-like, inftructed them in our arts both of war and peace, informed them of our ftrength and our weaknefs, and, at laft,—oh fhame!—compelled me to make a difgraceful retreat.

Valverde. But vengeance hovers over his head.

Pizarro. Yes! I have returned with a mightier force! and the boy fhall feel that Pizarro ftill lives!

Valverde. The queftion is,—whether Alonzo ftill lives?

Pizarro. That is certain. His follower, Diego, is juft taken prifoner, who reports the enemy to be twelve thoufand ftrong, with Alonzo and Rolla at their head. This day they offer a great facrifice to their idols;—Of the thoughtlefs fecurity of that moment I mean to take advantage, and fprinkle their facrifice with their own blood.

Elvira. Surprife!—battle!—Pizarro, will you not take me with you?

Pizarro. We are not going to a ball.

Elvira. Nor did I fuppofe I made the requeft to a dancer.

Pizarro. If you can find in my armoury, a fword light enough to fuit the hands of a woman, come and take your ftation at my fide.

Elvira. Shall you then love me better?

2　　　　　　　　　　　*Pizarro.*

Pizarro. Yes ; and for this reason ; because the tumult of battle would be a fortress in which I should confider your fidelity as fecure.

Elvira. You mistake A woman intent upon deceiving would not be deterred from her purpofe, even by ftorms or earthquakes.

Pizarro. I thank you for the hint; and will write it in my memory.

Elvira. You cannot write.

Pizarro. (*With a look of anger*) Elvira !

Elvira. Is that my fault?

Pizarro. You know, what I will not endure to hear.

Elvira. Had one of your legs been broken at nurfe ; fhould you have been afhamed of limping ?

Pizarro. Enough —let me never hear this again.

Elvira. (*Afide*) Achilles was vulnerable only in the heel.

SCENE III.—DIEGO *is brought in guarded.*

Pizarro. Behold Diego !—welcome, good friend.

Diego. Oh, me!—unfortunate mother's fon that I am !

Pizarro. Do you not recollect me ?

Diego. Could I poffibly forget the flower of Spanifh knighthood ?

Pizarro. How long may it be, fince you laft vifited my kitchen?

Diego. So long, that I am now almoft wafted to a fkeleton

Pizarro. Is your mafter living ?

Diego. He is.

Pizarro. What brought you into our camp ?

Diego. The people in your outpofts were roafting a fucking pig; and I was allured by the fmell.

Pizarro. What is the enemy's ftrength?

Diego. Twelve thoufand men.

Pizarro. And Alonzo is at their head?

Diego. Alonzo and Rolla.

Pizarro. Who is this Rolla ?

Diego. A favage in league with Satan himfelf. He flourifhes a club with the fame eafe as I might a quarter of lamb; and is as ready with the ufe of his fword, as your cook with her fkimmer.

Pizarro. I fhall be glad to become acquainted with him. Are he and Alonzo friends?

Diego. Warm friends; for he is in love with Donna Cora.

Elvira. Who is Donna Cora?

Diego. My mafter's wife.

Pizarro. Your mafter then is married?

Valverde. And to a heathen!—what an abomination!

Diego. But they love each other, like two common people.

Valverde. Has fhe been baptized?

Diego. No; for my mafter thinks that fhe may be virtuous without it.

Valverde. The mifcreant!

Pizarro. Is Cora with him in the camp?

Diego. Both fhe and her child, as well as a number of other women.

Pizarro. I rejoice to hear it. The more incumbrances they have among them, the eafier will be our victory; and befides the womens' cries and fcreams difhearten the men. Are they prepared for battle?

Diego. They are to have a great facrifice this day.

Valverde. To the Devil, I fuppofe?

Diego. No, to the Sun.

Valverde. A human facrifice, however?

Diego. Only fruits and aromatic plants.

Pizarro. It fhall be our part to fprinkle them with human blood.—Enough, Signor Diego. You, in the mean time, may ferve as turn-fpit in my kitchen.

Diego. Moft willingly. Look at my meagre body and lank legs. Putrid fifh, four cherries, and maize, are the only food which this country has afforded me.

Pizarro. The fate you deferve is, to be tied up to the next tree.

Diego. Oh terrible! (*To Elvira.*) Fair, young gentleman, intercede for me!

Pizarro. Be gone!—Thou oweft thy life to thy ftupidity.

C

Diego,

Diego. Then God be thanked for making me ftupid! (*Going*)

One of the Guards. Is he to be put in chains?

Diego. Fool! put thy own tongue in chains.

Pizarro. Give him plenty to eat and drink: then we fhall be fecure againft his running away.

Diego. Long live Don Pizarro!—he does not forget his old friends. (*Exit*)

Pizarro. Yes, it is refolved! the facrificers fhall become the victims. Firft we will hold a council of war; and then to battle. Elvira leave me.

Elvira. Why this command?

Pizarro. Becaufe I am going to hold counfel with men.

Elvira. As if a woman were then an intruder. Truly you men are ungrateful wretches:—you would employ the moft ufeful creature beftowed upon you by nature, merely as a play-thing. I will ftay.

Pizarro. Stay then; but be filent, if you can.

Elvira. I fhall be occupied in thought. It is only the empty head that babbles—reflection is always filent.

SCENE IV.—*Enter* LAS-CASAS, ALMAGRO, GON-ZALO, DAVILA, *and other* OFFICERS.

Las-Cafas. You have fummoned us hither.

Pizarro. Sit down venerable old men,—and you, my good friends. The moment is arrived in which we are to reap the fruits of our hazardous enterprize. The enemy, lulled in fecurity, this day offer a facrifice to their gods, at which moment, I am of opinion that we fhould furprize them, put the armed to death, and make the unarmed flaves.

Almagro. My voice is for death to every Peruvian, armed or unarmed.

Gonzalo. But, we may fpare the women and children.

Almagro. Better extirpate the whole race.

Valverde. For the honour of our faith!

Las-Cafas. Do not blafpheme.

I

Almagro.

Almagro. We have loitered a sufficient time upon this coast.

Las-Casas. And you would have recourse to murder, for employment.

Almagro. We are as yet unrepaid for the heavy expences of our armament.

Pizarro. We are reduced to want, and the troops begin to murmur.

Gonzalo. While Alonzo, rioting in abundance, scoffs at us.

Pizarro. Traiterous boy!

Las Casas. My heart whispers me, that Alonzo feels a painful conflict in his bosom, between humanity and love for his native country.

Almagro. Your heart seeks to defend your pupil.

Las-Casas. Yes, he is indeed my pupil, and I am proud to call him so!

Almagro. Enough?—he shall learn to know us.

Pizarro. The enemy's force increases every day; we are strangers to the country, surrounded by want, and delay relaxes courage. The only resource against such numerous and formidable evils, is a battle.

All. (*Excepting Las-Casas*) A battle!—a battle!

Las Casas. What a re-echoing of that dreadful word! —And against whom is this attack to be directed?—against a mild king, who but a few days ago offered you his hand in peace—against a people, whom you found inoffensively tilling their fields, and with innocent hearts worshipping their Creator, according to their own form.

Valverde. Heathens who adore the Sun, and whom the sword must extirpate.

Las-Casas. Is the bloody measure of your barbarities not yet full?—When will you be satiated with the sufferings of these pious children of innocence, who received you so hospitably?—Thou Power Almighty, whose thunder cleaves the rocks, and whose Sun can dissolve even mountains of ice, lend thy force to my words, since it is my glory I seek to uphold! (*Addressing himself again to the Almighty,*) Oh cast but a retrospective glance upon the millions of unhappy victims already sacrificed to your rapacity!—You were received by this people as gods, you came among them as devils!—Willingly and

C 2   cheerfully

cheerfully did they give you of their gold and fruits, while,
in return, you violated their wives and daughters.—Human
nature revolted against such outrages, and the oppressed
began to utter complaints—then, did you send your blood
hounds to hunt them down, while those who escaped from
this infernal chace, were either yoked to the plough to cul-
tivate their own fields for your use, or buried in their
gold mines, to supply your insatiable avarice with the precious ore.

Pizarro.   You exaggerate!

Las-Casas.   I exaggerate!—Would to God that this
were all! but more still remains—deeds that might draw
tears from the eyes of a tyger!—Yet, Oh my sorrows!
overpower me not, permit me to speak on!—Wagers
were laid among you, which could cleave a man asunder, or
strike off a head with the greatest dexterity—you tore
children from their mother's arms, and dashed them against
rocks—you roasted the chiefs at a slow fire, and if their
dreadful cries disturbed the slumbers of the dæmons by
whom they were tormented, gags were thrust into their
throats to silence them.   Thirteen Indians were hung
upon thirteen separate gibbets—Oh God! can it be men-
tioned without blaspheming!—in honour of Christ and his
Apostles!—These horrors, my own eyes have witnessed
and I still live!—Donna Elvira, you weep—is your heart
alone affected by this horrible picture?

Almagro.   She and you are the only women among us.

Pizarro.   What you relate does not concern us.   We
are not responsible for the barbarities of a Columbus, or
an Ovando.

Las-Casas.   Are you not about to renew them?

Valverde.   Supposing we were—it remains yet undecid-
ed, whether these Indians be men or apes.

Las-Casas.   Woe unto those who wait for a Bull from
the Holy-Father, before they can decide such a ques-
tion.

Valverde.   The new world was given us by him, " *to
subdue it by aid of the divine favour.*' *

---

* The words of the Papal Bull.   See Robertson's History of
America.   *Note by the Author.*

Pizarro.

Pizarro. Enough of this war of words. Time paſſes, and opportunity flies—are you reſolved to fight?

All. 'Tis our earneſt deſire.

Las-Caſas. Oh ſend me firſt among theſe Peruvians, as a meſſenger of peace!—let me endeavour, by gentle means, to inſtil our holy religion into their hearts!

Valverde. Firſt, let our heroes fight, and prepare the way for your doctrines.

Las-Caſas. With blood?

Almagro. Which you may waſh away with pious tears! —Haſten my friends!—let us delay no longer!

Las-Caſas. O God! thou haſt anointed me thy ſervant, not to curſe, but to bleſs!—yet here my bleſſing were blaſphemy!—Be ye curſed then, ye fratricides!—curſed be your barbarous projects, and may the innocent blood ſhed this day, be upon you, and your children!—For me, I renounce your ſociety for ever.—I can no longer endure to be a witneſs of your ſavage phrenzy. I will bury my-ſelf in ſome cave or foreſt, and hold intercourſe only with thoſe leſs ferocious monſters, tygers and leopards—and when, at laſt, I ſhall ſtand in judgment, together with you, before him whoſe mild doctrines you have this day for-ſworn, then, tremble at the charges I muſt be compelled to bring againſt you!—(*Going*)

Elvira. (*With involuntary emotion*) Las-Caſas, take me with you!

Las-Caſas. No, remain here, and, if it be poſſible, ſave theſe men from the judgments which their inhumanity muſt call down upon them. I can go no farther—my efforts are exhauſted—but the charms of a woman may prove more powerful than the eloquence of an old man. Perhaps you may be elected as the guardian angel of theſe unfortunate Peruvians. (*Exit*)

Pizarro. What would you do, Elvira?

Elvira. I ſcarcely know, myſelf. Las-Caſas appeared to me at this moment, like ſomething more than human; and you with all the reſt, ſo far below humanity—

Almagro. The old man raves.

Valverde. And plans viſionary worlds, like Plato.

Pizarro. He has no longer any powers of enjoyment himſelf, himfelf, and therefore affumes the character of a preacher of repentance.

Elvira. Say what you pleafe; but my heart revolts againft your proceedings.

Gonzalo. Compaffion is becoming to a beautiful woman.

Elvira. As humanity to a conqueror.

Pizarro. It is well, that we are rid of this preacher of morality.

Almagro. We fhall now yawn lefs, and fight more.

Pizarro. At noon, the enemy will be engaged in this facrifice; then, Almagro, you fhall wheel round by the left, through the foreft, while you, Gonzalo, fhall afcend the hill to the right, and I will fall upon the camp directly in front. If we fucceed here, the gates of Quito are opened to receive us.

Almagro. And we hail thee, our general, king of Peru.

Pizarro. Excufe me, my good friends. He who proceeds flowly, proceeds fecurely. Ataliba fhall remain on his throne, the fhadow of a fovereign, while I will marry his daughter, govern under him, and fecure my fucceffion to the monarchy at his death.

Gonzalo. An excellent plan.

Almagro. Pizarro is alike the hero and the ftatefman.

Valverde. (*Afide to Elvira, farcaftically*) Now, Elvira!

Elvira. A very excellent plan!—And what is to become of Elvira?

Pizarro. She fhall continue with her friend.

Elvira. As a fervant in the royal palace?

Pizarro. I fhall give the heirefs of Peru, what is commonly given to Princeffes, my hand;—but my heart will ftill be Elvira's.

Elvira. And when fhe advances in years, you will make her governefs to your children?—Am I not right?

Pizarro. You are offended, Elvira. But, recollect, that a throne is in queftion.

Elvira. Offended!—no, I am only provoked, that this ftupid fellow fhould underftand Pizarro's character better than myfelf.

Pizarro. What do you mean?

Elvira. Nothing!—mere fancies!—Forgive this feminine

minine loquacity ; it fhall no longer interfere with the valiant deeds of thefe heroes.—Away ! the din of arms fum-
mons you hence !—hafte, hafte, ye mighty champions !

Pizarro. You will accompany us ?

Elvira. Certainly!—to be the firft who fhall pay homage
to the king's new fon-in-law.

SCENE V.—*Enter* GOMEZ.

Almagro. What brings you hither, Gomez ?

Gomez. I come to announce a prifoner whom we have
taken. Beneath a palm-tree upon yonder hill, we found
an old Cazique, lurking apparently, as a fpy upon our
camp. He could not efcape, therefore furrendered without
refiftance ; yet every word he utters, is full of reproach
and contempt.

Pizarro. Bring him hither. (*Exit Gomez, who returns
immediately with the Cazique*) Who are you ?

Cazique. (*With perfect tranquillity, devoid of oftentation*)
Which is the chief of this band of robbers ?

Pizarro. Ha !

Almagro. Art thou frantic ? (*To Pizarro*) Tear out
his tongue.

Cazique. Are you fo much afraid of hearing the truth ?

Davila. (*Drawing out a dagger*) Suffer me to plunge
this into his heart ?

Cazique. (*To Pizarro*) Have you many fuch heroes in
your army ?

Pizarro. Headftrong fool, thou fhalt die !—but, firft,
confefs all that thou knoweft.

Cazique. That is already done. But one thing I have
this moment learned from you.

Pizarro. And what is that ?

Cazique. That I fhall die.

Pizarro. By abating in this ftubbornnefs, thy life might
be faved.

Cazique.

Cazique. My remainder of life is like a withered tree, not worth preferving.

Pizarro. Our arms might raife you to the highest rank among your own people.

Cazique. My countrymen are not unacquainted with old Crozimbo! he never was one of the loweft among them.

Pizarro. We intend, this morning, to fall upon your army by furprize. Be you our guide through the foreft, and you fhall be loaded with treafures.

Cazique. Ha! ha! ha!

Pizarro. You laugh?

Cazique. I am already a rich man. I have two valiant fons, who will fhed the laft drop of their blood for their country; and have befides, the fweet confcioufnefs of having performed many good actions.

Pizarro. What is the ftrength of your army?

Cazique. Number the trees in the foreft.

Almagro. Which is the weakeft fide of your camp?

Cazique. The juftice of our caufe protects it on all fides.

Davila. At what hour will your king offer his facrifice to the Sun?

Cazique. Our thanks and praifes are offered to him at all hours.

Pizarro. Where are your women and children concealed?

Cazique. In the hearts of their hufbands and fathers.

Almagro. Do you know Alonzo?

Cazique. Do I know him?—The benefactor of our nation!

Pizarro. How has he deferved that appellation?

Cazique. By not refembling you in any feature of his character.

Almagro. Madman! fpeak more refpectfully!

Cazique. I fpeak truth to God; fhall I be afraid to fpeak it to man?

Valverde. You do not know God.

Cazique. (*Extending his arms towards heaven with pious confidence*) Yes, I do know him!

Valverde. The religion which we bring you, is the only true religion.

Cazique.

Cazique. That is written in our hearts.

Valverde. Ye are Idolaters.

Cazique. Leave us to follow our ancient faith, which has taught us to live happy, and die content.

Davila. Obdurate race!

Cazique. Young robber, we plunder no one of his property.

Davila. Be filent or tremble.

Cazique. I never trembled before God ;—fhall I tremble before man ?—before thee, thou lefs than man ?

Davila. *(Drawing a dagger)* Not another word, heathen dog ; or this dagger fhall difpatch thee.

Cazique. Difpatch me ;—and then you will be able to boaft, that you alfo have killed a Peruvian.

Davila. *(Stabbing him)* Hence, to hell !

Pizarro. What have you done ?

Davila. Could you endure any longer to liften to his revilings ?

Pizarro. Ought he to have died without torture ?

Cazique. Young man, you have loft a noble opportunity of learning to fuffer patiently.

Elvira. Barbarians ! *(She bends down to the Cazique)* Poor old man !

Cazique. Call me not poor, when I am fo near my happinefs. Ha ! my wife beckons me !—The fun fmiles upon me '—God amend—and blefs you ! *(Dies)*

Elvira. Valverde, could a Chriftian make a better end?

Valverde. He was ftrengthened by Satan.

Pizarro. Drag the body hence !—And you, Davila, be not again fo over-hafty.

Davila. Pardon me ; I could not reftrain my indignation.

Pizarro. Follow me, friends ; and let every one haften to his appointed poft. Before the God of Peru fhall fink again into the ocean, the walls of Quito muft be overturown. *(Exit, followed by Almagre, Gonzalo, Davila, Gomez, and others)*

SCENE VI.—*Manent only* ELVIRA *and* VALVERDE.

Valverde. Lovely Elvira! my hopes increase with Pizarro's increased haughtiness.

Elvira. Oh! how painfully my mind is agitated!—These horrible variations in scenes of barbarity!—this shameful avowal of avarice and ambition!—

Valverde. Throw yourself into my arms!

Elvira. Wretched, indeed, were my lot, had I no other resource but to throw myself into Valverde's arms!

Valverde. Do you not think me capable of aiming the stroke of a dagger with certainty?

Elvira. Not if you were to face the man. But, tell me,—at what price would you value a murder?

Valverde. At a very high price; though easy to be paid.

Elvira. You mistake. Yet, an injured woman can scarcely purchase revenge at too dear a rate. Go,—leave me.—You shall hear from me again.

Valverde. The dagger is whetted, the arm raised;—one word only,—and he lies bleeding at your feet. [*Exit.*

SCENE VII.—ELVIRA *alone.*

No!—even if my soul did entertain projects of murder, I would not seek it in such a way, nor through the medium of such an instrument. Enter into a compact with this despicable wretch!—hateful idea!—If Pizarro should, indeed, thrust me from his bosom; spurn one who has sacrificed to him her honour, her virtue!—then!——Spurn me!—No; I will spurn him!—What part of his character was it that engaged my love?—his supposed greatness!—He is become contemptible,—and that love is extinguished!—Yet, hold! —Does a man always execute whatever he resolves?—Ambition builds houses of cards, and love blows them down. Prove him, therefore, once more Elvira; and if he still appear unworthy of thee,—then trample him in the dust from which he rose. [*Exit.*

END OF THE FIRST ACT.

ACT II.

SCENE I.—*The Peruvian Camp near a Village.   On the Middle of the Stage is an Altar—in the Back Ground a Hill, on which stands a Palm-Tree.*

CORA *sits upon a Bank of Turf, with her Child in her Arms;* ALONZO *stands by, and looks at her with a Countenance expressive of great Delight and Affection.* CORA *observes, first him, then the Child, with Smiles of Extasy.*

CORA.

HE is very like you.

Alonzo.   No, like you.

Cora.   Oh! do not deprive me of my favourite idea!

Alonzo.   Has he not black hair?

Cora.   But blue eyes.

Alonzo.   And is not his smile exactly like your's?

Cora.   (Pressing the child to her bosom)   He is equally like both.

Alonzo.   Since you have had the child playing on your lap, the father has lost a portion of your love.

Cora.   Do not say so.

Alonzo.   He steals many kisses from you, which are mine by right.

Cora.

Cora. I kifs you in him.

Alonzo. The boy will make me jealous.

Cora. I live only in you and him. I dreamed laft night, that the white bloffoms of his teeth were beginning to appear.

Alonzo. That day fhall be celebrated as a feftival.

Cora. And when he fhall run from me to you—

Alonzo. And lifp, father, mother—

Cora. Oh, Alonzo, our daily thanks fhould be offered to the gods.

Alonzo. To them and Rolla.

Cora. You are happy?—are you not?

Alonzo. Can Cora make that a queftion?

Cora. Why then are you fo often reftlefs at night?—and why does your bofom fo often heave with mournful fighs?

Alonzo. Are not thefe men, againft whom I muft fight, my brethren?

Cora. All men are equally your brethren; and is not our deftruction, the aim of thefe Spaniards?

Alonzo. Should they prove victorious, what a fate awaits me!

Cora. We would feek refuge among the mountains.

Alonzo. How could you fly with a child in your arms?

Cora. Think you that a mother, anxious for her child's fafety, is ever fenfible of its weight?

Alonzo. And I can help you to bear the fweet burthen.

Cora. He will not be quiet with you.

Alonzo. Dear Cora, would you wifh to make me tranquil?

Cora. Oh, moft truly!

Alonzo. Then haften, this very hour, to the mountains, to your father. There you will be fafe; and when the conteft fhall be ended, I will follow you, either to announce our victory, or that we may pafs the remainder of our days together, in that afylum of nature.

Cora. Where we will educate our fon as an avenger of his country's wrongs.

Alonzo. Yes, that fhall be our chief bufinefs and delight.

Cora. Yet, fpare me, Alonzo, I cannot go at this

Cora.

moment. How could I bear to be abfent from you in the hour of danger?—How endure the idea, that you, perhaps, were wounded, and left to the care of others.

Alonzo. Will not Rolla remain with me?

Cora. Only during the battle. Rolla underftands well how to inflict wounds, but knows little about curing them. —Should you fall, he will revenge your death, but he would not fnatch you from impending danger. No, wherever the hufband is, there fhou'd the wife be alfo.—I fwore never to forfake you, even in death.

Alonzo. Oh, mirror of conftancy!—Remain here then and heaven grant us victory!

Cora. Reflect, Alonzo, that on our fide the conteft is folely for our own defence;—affuredly, the gods will grant us their protection.

Alonzo. If not, death will find me encompaffed by your arms.

Cora. Talk not of death. Since I have been poffeffed of thee and my Fernando; I cannot bear to think of him.

Alonzo. (*On his knees, embracing his wife and child*) Adored wife, born to blefs me, and almoft by a miracle mine. —how unfortunate is he, who in fearching after happinefs, overlooks love.

Cora. (*Returning his careffes*) Love is a filent and fequeftered being, not to be difcovered by thofe who delight in noife and tumult

Alonzo. My Cora!—my world!

Cora. My Alonzo!—my all!

SCENE II.—*Enter* ROLLA, *unperceived by them.* He *paufes a few moments, to obferve their careffes.*

Rolla. The gods be thanked for fo grateful a fight!

Alonzo: Ha, Rolla!—you here!

Rolla. I was fharing your tranfports.

Alonzo. 'Tis to you we owe them.

Rolla. How fweet a reflection to my heart.

Cora.

Cora. Dear Rolla, you have made me inexpreſſibly happy.

Rolla. Corà happy through Rolla's means!—Ye monarchs of the earth, is there one among you, with whom I would exchange ſituations?

Alonzo. Our brother!

Cora. More than brother—our friend!

Rolla. Go on, go on,—exalt me above myſelf—let me revel in your happineſs.

Cora. Should this child love you leſs than his father, he will incur his mother's curſe.

Rolla. In all that I have done, my ſole objeƈt was to promote Cora's happineſs—ſhe is happy, and I am repaid. At preſent take the counſel of a friend— retire with your child farther into the foreſt, or among the mountains; there you will be in greater ſafety.

Alonzo. I have urged her to do this, but hitherto in vain.

Cora. Can I be unſafe with Rolla and Alonzo?

Rolla. The enemy meditate a ſurprize.—

Cora. And ſhould that be attempted —are we not ſufficiently guarded againſt it?

Rolla. The diſpoſal of viƈtory reſts ſtill with God.

Cora. We can eaſily, if neceſſary, fly together.

Alonzo. Spare yourſelf the anguiſh you muſt experience amid the tumult of battle.

Cora. I can feel anguiſh only at a diſtance from you.

Rolla. You cannot aſſiſt, and may injure us.

Cora. Injure you! how can that be?

Rolla. Muſt I ſpeak more plainly?—you know how much we love you.—If you remain near us, we ſhall fight with inexpreſſible anxiety, and be continually turning towards the place where you are ſtationed. A lover can never be a complete general, unleſs he knows the beloved objeƈt to be at a diſtance, and in ſafety.

Alonzo. Rolla is in the right. How could I ruſh boldly among the enemy, while I beheld a Spaniard near me, who might preſs onwards, and deprive me of my Cora?

Cora. You may ſeek to bribe the vanity of a woman— but the wife hears you not.

Alonzo. And is the mother equally inſenſible to our entreaties?

Rolla.

Rolla. Act as will beft fatisfy yourfelf, I have urged only what I feel to be right.

Alonzo. All our women are concealed, yourfelf alone excepted.

Cora. I have the firmeft reliance upon you and the gods, yet, for your fatisfaction, I will go whitherfoever you pleafe.

Alonzo. Deareft wife, accept my thanks!

Rolla. The king is coming to the facrifice.

Alonzo. Are we properly fecured againft a furprize?

Rolla. All our out-pofts are vigilantly guarded.

Alonzo. I have miffed Diego. I do not believe that he would defignedly betray us; but he is both a fool and a coward?

Rolla. Be under no apprehenfions; we are prepared for every thing.

SCENE III. — *Enter* ATALIBA, *with a long train of* PRIESTS, COURTIERS, SOLDIERS, *and* WOMEN.

Ataliba. Welcome, Alonzo!—your hand, brave Rolla! (*To Cora*) The gods blefs thee, happy mother!

Cora. May the gods blefs the father of his people!

Ataliba. To fee his children happy, is the choiceft blefling to a father. My friends, how ftand the fpirits of our brave troops?

Alonzo. They fhout in tranfport, " *Our king is among us!*"

Rolla. " *He fhares our toils and dangers.*"

Alonzo. " *God and the king!*"

Rolla. " *Victory or death!*"

Ataliba. I know my people—know that, were this fhield pierced through, every fubject would offer his breaft as a fhield.

Alonzo. When, I hope, the Inca would chufe mine.

Rolla. And not neglect Rolla's.

Cora.

Cora. (*Holding up her child*) Behold here a champion growing up for your fon !

Ataliba. Your love is my choiceft treafure, and in that I feel myfelf rich. But fay, do the enemy ftill remain quiet ?

Rolla. They do.—Yet their repofe feems like the filence of the gathering thunder-cloud.

Ataliba. Be tranquil courage our fhelter from the ftorm.

Rolla. They fight for defpicable gold, we for our native country.

Alonzo. An adventurer leads them to battle, we are led on by a fovereign whom we love.

Ataliba. And a god whom we adore ! — Come, my friends, to him let our facrifice be offered !

(*The Priefts range themfelves behind the Altar, the King and the reft of the Affembly on each fide of it.*)

CHORUS OF PRIESTS.*

Thou God who gav'ft us being, fmile
Benignly on our pious toil !

THE PEOPLE.

Oh may the childrens' lifping fong,
The youths', which firmer flows along,
The old-mens' feebly utter'd ftrain,
May *all*, thy kind acceptance gain !
And may'ft thou twine an everlafting band
Between our fovereign and his native land !

CHORUS OF PRIESTS.

Ye children of the radiant fun, kneel down
And make, by prayers and fongs, your homage known.

* Thefe Choruffes are verfified by the fame Friend to whom the Tranflator was obliged for the verfification of thofe in the " *Virgin of the Sun.*"

THE PEOPLE (*Kneeling*).

Our hearts from impious thoughts, Oh God, are free !
And here, thofe hearts we offer up to thee !

(*The King approaches the altar, and ftrews upon it, fruits
and aromatic herbs ; while the Priefts fing with uplifted
hands.*)

CHORUS OF PRIESTS.

Oh God, on us fend down thy rays !
   And if accepted ftrains we fing,
   Be the pure offering which we bring
Confum'd before us, by the facred blaze !

(*Fire defcends from Heaven, and confumes the facrifice.*)

THE PEOPLE.

Rejoice ! rejoice ! hence ev'ry fear !
The God has deign'd our vows to hear.
Behold the facrifice confum'd !——
Then be the murd'rous fword refum'd ;
Hafte, point th' unerring arrow high,
For us fhall vict'ry's banners fly.
Rejoice ! rejoice ! hence ev'ry fear !
The God has deign'd our vows to hear.

SCENE IV.—*Enter an* INDIAN *almoft breathlefs.*

Indian.   The enemy——
Ataliba.   Are they near ?
Rolla.   Which way do they advance ?
Indian.   I furveyed their camp from the top of the hill,
and faw the whole army in motion.
Rolla.   Enough.

             E   *Ataliba*

THE SPANIARDS IN PERU; OR,

Ataliba. Let the women and children be conveyed to a place of safety.

Cora. Oh! Alonzo!

Alonzo. We shall soon meet again.

Cora. Bless your son.

Alonzo. God protect both you and him!

Ataliba. Haste! the moments are precious.

(The women cling round the necks of their husbands, the children clasp the knees of their fathers)

Alonzo. *(To Cora)* Oh, go! ere my fortitude be wholly overpowered!

Cora. I obey. Prove yourself a hero—but hazard not your life without necessity.

Rolla. Will not Cora say one word to Rolla?

Cora. Take my hand, dear Rolla—bring me back Alonzo.

Ataliba. The gods protect both you and us!

Cora. And grant us to meet again in safety!

    [*Exit Cora, together with the Priests, the women, and the children.*

Ataliba. *(Drawing his sword)* Away, my friends!

Rolla. We are ready.

Ataliba. You, Alonzo, shall defend the narrow pass in the mountains;—you, Rolla, receive the enemy to the right, in the forest;—I will remain in the centre, and fight till I fall.

Rolla. You fall not without us.

Ataliba. You must live for my son's sake; and train him up to avenge his country's wrongs.

Alonzo. Victory to our legal father!

Rolla. In the evening we will return thanks to the gods.

Ataliba. The cry is—GOD AND OUR NATIVE COUNTRY!—[*Exit Ataliba.--Rolla is about to follow him; but is detained by Alonzo.*

Alonzo. Yet one word, Rolla.

Rolla. To arms—is the word! *(Going.)*

Alonzo. One word of Cora.

Rolla. Of Cora!—speak!

Alonzo. What must the next hour bring us?

Rolla. Victory, or death!

Alonzo. Victory perhaps to you, death to me. Perhaps the reverse--who can tell?

                          Rolla.

Rolla. Or both may fall.

Alonzo. If fo, my wife and child are left to God and the king. God will confole, the king protect them.

Rolla. Moft certainly.

Alonzo. But, fhould I alone fall, then, Rolla, be you my heir !

Rolla. What do you mean ?

Alonzo. Take Cora as your wife, my child as your own,

Rolla. Be it fo !

Alonzo. Your hand upon it.

Rolla. But not without Cora's free confent.

Alonzo. Tell her it was my laft wifh.

Rolla. I will.

Alonzo. And carry my blefling to her and my fon.

Rolla. Enough !—In the hour of battle I had rather liften to the drum, than to the laft will of a hufband and father.

Alonzo. I know not whence proceed thefe melancholy forebodings, but I never felt fo fad at heart.

Rolla. Away then to the field.

Alonzo. Yet one word more. Should this hour prove, indeed my laft, let my body be interred beneath the palm-tree, under whofe fhade we have fo often fpent our evenings. Then continue the fame practice; fo will you fit with Cora upon the grave of your friend ; fo fhall my fpirit be ftill among you, while on each flower that my child plucks from the hallowed earth, fhall a tear be dropped to the memory of your departed friend, and each zephyr that whifpers among the leaves, fhall be echoed with a refponfive figh.

Rolla. Away, away, with thefe fancies !

Alonzo. No, let me cherifh them !—let me indulge in the fond hope, that you ftill will think of me !

Rolla. Can you doubt that ?

Alonzo. Now to battle.

Rolla. You to the left,—I to the right—we fhall meet again.

Alonzo. In heaven, if not on earth.

Rolla. On earth !—on earth!

Alonzo. Heaven grant it !

Rolla. Let us draw our fwords. *(They both draw them.)*

E 2 *Alonzo.*

Alonzo. For the King and Cora !
Rolla. For Cora and the King !

     [*Exeunt on different fides.*

SCENE V.—*Manent. only a* blind OLD MAN, *and a*
   BOY.

Old Man. Are they gone ?
Boy. Yes, all difperfed.
Old Man. Alas, my eyes !—Had I retained my fight,
I might ftill have grafped a fword, and died honourably.
Boy. Shall I lead you home ?
Old Man. No, my child ; lead me to the altar. *(The
boy leads him thither)* Here let me ftand. Are we quite
alone ?
Boy. They are all gone ; father and mother too. Fa-
ther is gone with the foldiers,—but I don't know what's
become of mother.
Old Man. I am uneafy about you, poor child !
Boy. I can ftay with you, dear grandfather.
Old Man. But what would you do, fhould the enemy
come ?
Boy. I will tell them, that you are old and blind.
Old Man. They will drag you away.
Boy. No, grandfather ; for they will fee plainly that
you cannot walk without me to guide you. *(A noife is
heard at a diftance.)*
Old Man. Hark ! the battle is already begun !—Go,
child, get upon your grandmother's grave, whence you
can climb up the tree that I planted at its foot. It is already fo tall, that, when you are at the top, you will be
able to fee over the field of battle.
Boy. Shall I leave you here alone ?
Old Man. I will reft againft the altar; God will protect me. Go, and tell me what you hear and fee. *(The
boy climbs up the tree.)* Since I learned the ufe of arms, this
is the firft battle in which I have not borne a part. A few
years ago, I could bend the bow, or throw the lance with not
          lefs

lefs dexterity than the Inca himfelf;—now, alas ! I can only
pull cotton with the women ;—can only liften to the din of
arms, and the clafhing of fhields; but can neither help
others nor myfelf. Yet, every time the fhout of battle
meets my ears—every time I hear the found of martial in-
ftruments—I clench my hand with involuntary ardour,
and grafp at the fide whence I was accuftomed to draw my
fword—but ah ! no fword is to be found !—Well, child,
what do you fee ?

Boy. A great deal of duft and fmoke !

Old Man. How often have I been enveloped in fuch a
duft !—how often fwallowed it in abundance!—The
fmoke muft doubtlefs proceed from the dreadful fire-arms
of the Spaniards, which roar and vomit flames, like the
fearful mountain of Catacunga.—What elfe do you fee,
child ?

Boy. When the fmoke feparates, I can fee our people.

Old Man. Do they pufh forwards?

Boy. No, they ftand.

Old Man. That, however, is good.—Do you fee the
ftandard of the Inca's?

Boy. Yes, it is waving in the midft of them.

Old Man. Thanks to the gods !—The king then is
ftill unhurt.

Boy. Now I can fee the enemy alfo ;—their arms
glitter.

Old Man. What elfe?—what elfe do you fee ?

Boy. The enemy are not like our people.

Old Man. How, how do they differ ?

Boy. They are a vaft deal larger, and move as quick
again.

Old Man. Pooh, pooh, child!—they ride upon large
and fpirited animals.

Boy. Now they mix among our Peruvians.

Old Man. And fall, I hope ?

Boy. There is fo much fmoke and lightning !

Old Man. Thou avenging God! fend thy lightning
down from the clouds to their confufion and difmay !

Boy. The ftandard of the Incas difappears.

Old Man. Oh miferable !

Boy. Our people give way.

Old Man. My fword !—my fword !—I will go !—I
will fight '—Oh glorious Sun ! let me but once more behold thy rays !

Boy.

Boy. And now, a thick cloud conceals them all.

Old Man. Woe is me, that I fhould live to fee the day when I can no longer ferve my native country!—Yet, at leaft, I can affift it with my prayers! (*He kneels, and clafps the altar*) Ye gods, who bow us down, oh ceafe to withhold your favour from a people who honour you with perfect purity and fincerity!—Protect your fervant, our good Inca, and fuffer him not to fall by the hands of robbers!

Boy. A fmall troop are coming this way.

Old Man. Are they enemies?

Boy. I can fee nothing but duft.

Old Man. Away, good child, haften to the mountains!

Boy. I fee the points of lances glitter.

Old Man. Then they are Peruvians.

Boy. They come this way.

Old Man. Defcend from the tree, my child.

Boy. All feem mixed together at a diftance.

Old Man. But our people ftill fight?

Boy. They give way flowly.

Old Man. Yet they do give way!—Oh ye cruel gods! —My child, come down!

Boy. (*Defcending fram the tree*) Shall we look for mother?

Old Man. No, my child. Alas! I fear we muft look only to the grave!

SCENE VI. *Enter* ATALIBA *wounded, he is fupported by fome of his Soldiers.*

Ataliba. Here let me reft!—here die, if death muft be my lot!

A Soldier. We will remain with you.

Ataliba. Oh, no! return to the battle; your fervices are wanted.

Soldier. But your wound——

Ataliba. Is not dangerous. Go, revenge your fallen brethren: go, I command you! [*Exeunt the Soldiers.*

(*Ataliba*

(*Ataliba leans against the altar*) Ye righteous gods! how have I deserved this chastisement?

Old Man. I hear the voice of lamentation; but I cannot see the sufferer. Who is it that complains thus?

Ataliba. A forsaken wretch, whose only resource is in death.

Old Man. Is the king still alive?

Ataliba. He is.

Old Man. Then you cannot be forsaken. Ataliba protects even the lowest among his subjects.

Ataliba. And who protects him?

Old Man. The gods.

Ataliba. Their anger has fallen heavily upon him.

Old Man. That cannot be. He has never oppressed the weak; never refused justice to any one; never pampered his courtiers upon the sweat of his peasants; never closed his hand against the needy; nor denied a hearing to just complaints.

Ataliba. (*Aside*) Oh, God! what sensations of transport dost thou mingle with these bitterest moments of my life!—Good old man, do you know the king?

Old Man. Extremely well:—I have often seen him. It is not many years since I fought by his side, against Huascar.

Ataliba. How long were you in the service?

Old Man. Fifty-four years.

Ataliba. And has such fidelity never been rewarded?

Old Man. Do I not enjoy repose in the bosom of my family?

Ataliba. But that is the only reward you have received?

Old Man. And is that a trifle?—Oh! what has not a king accomplished who has secured happiness to his subjects!

Ataliba. He owed more to you.

Old Man. Do not say so. I hear, daily, from my grandchildren, of the blessings he diffuses among his people. I hear it with devout satisfaction, and rejoice!

Ataliba. (*Much affected*) And do all your brethren think the same?

Old Man. It is the general sentiment.

Ataliba. Why should I fear death?—How is it that I no longer feel my wound?

Old Man. Are you wounded?—Go, child, run to my hut, and fetch the balfam.   [*Exit the boy.*

Ataliba. I thank you moft fincerely.

Old Man. But you fhould not have quitted the king.

Ataliba. One of the tendons of my right arm is cut through—I could not fight any longer.

Old Man. You might have taken the fword in your left hand.

SCENE VII.—*Several* INDIANS *run over the ftage, as if purfued by the enemy.*

The Indians. All is loft!—fly!—fave yourfelf!

Ataliba. (*To one of the laft*) Stop, I command you! (*The man obeys*) Where is Alonzo?

Indian. I have not feen him.

Ataliba. Where is Rolla?

Indian. In the midft of the enemy.

Ataliba. And you have deferted your General?

Indian. (*With confufion*) I have loft my fword.

Ataliba. Take mine, and die worthy of a Peruvian.

Indian. Death alone fhall deprive me of fuch a prefent. (*He brandifhes the fword, and haftens back to the fight*)

Old Man. (*Calling after him*) Is the king fafe?—Alas! he does not hear me!

Ataliba. The king is ftill alive.

(*An Indian feverely wounded, ftaggers in with difficulty, and drops at the king's feet*)

Indian. Here let me die!

Ataliba. Is all loft?

Indian. All.

Ataliba. And is Rolla fallen?

Indian. No, he was ftill defending himfelf; but I faw Alonzo fall.

Ataliba. Alonzo fall!—Oh God!

Old Man. You do not enquire after the king.

Ataliba. (*Taking the fword from the wounded man*) Give me your fword, you can no longer ufe it.

Indian. My king, what would you do?

Ataliba,

Ataliba. Embitter the triumph of our enemies—bury myfelf among the ruins of my kingdom.

Old Man. Oh God! are you then Ataliba?

Ataliba. Let them come; I am prepared.

(Rolla's voice is heard at a diftance) Faint-hearted wretches!—ftop!—ftop!—return!—affemble round me! —'tis Rolla calls!

Several voices together. Rolla!—our father Rolla! Yes, we will rally round him!

Rolla. *(At a greater diftance.)* For God and the king! —Back, back, I fay!—back to the fight!

Ataliba. My brave Rolla, then, is alive!—I ftill have hopes.

Old Man. Good king, I knew not that you were fo near me. I am a poor, blind, old man.

Ataliba. Venerable foldier, your attachment has foothed me in an hour of wretchednefs.

Old Man. *(Having received the balfam from the boy)* Suffer my trembling hand to drop fome of this precious balfam into your wound, and then to bind it up.

Ataliba. I thank thee, truly.

Old Man. Oh that I had more to offer than this and my prayers!—Go, child, climb the tree once more. *(The boy climbs the tree.)*

The wounded Indian. *(Clafping Ataliba's foot, at which he has continued to lie)* Firft-born of the Sun—blefs me! —I die!—

Ataliba. For thy country!—God blefs and reward thee!

Indian. And God—blefs—our good—king—*(Dies.)*

Ataliba. Blood of my fubjects!—precious pledge entrufted to my care!—I have not fhed thee wantonly!

Old Man. Child, what do you fee?

Boy. Friends and enemies mingled together.

Old Man. Which give way?

Boy. Neither.

Ataliba. Ye gods! if your anger require fome atone-ment, ftrike here—but fpare, oh fpare, my people!

Boy. I fee feveral hats with plumes of feathers fall.

Old Man. They are the Spaniards. Strike, ftrike, ye brave fellows!—ftrike home!

F

Boy.

Boy. I fee Rolla.

Ataliba. He ſtands firmly?

Boy. His ſword flaſhes like lightning—it ſeems every where.

Old Man. He is the darling of the gods.

Ataliba. Of gods and men.

Boy. They give way!

Old Man. Who? who?

Boy. The enemy.

Old Man. Now it will do!—no relaxing—there lies one—there another!—puſh over the bodies—no compaſſion—ſee how they fall!—right!—right!—drive on!

Ataliba. What youthful ardour!

Boy. They fly!

Old Man. (Leaving the altar.) Ha! they fly!—purſue them!—extirpate the whole race!—Where am I?—Boy!—where am I?---

Boy. (With a great ſhout.) They fly!---they fly!

Ataliba. (Falling on his knees before the altar.) Oh God! my confidence is repaid!

Boy. (Coming down from the tree.) I ſaw plainly that they were flying, and the ſtandard of the Incas waved again. *(He leads his grandfather back to the altar)*

Old Man. Firſt born of the Sun! ſuffer me to kiſs thy hand!---a tear forces itſelf into my eyes—it is a tear of joy!---Firſt-born of the Sun! ſuffer me to weep upon thy hand!

Ataliba. (Riſing and giving him his hand.) Let us offer our thanks to the gods.

Old Man. Tears of joy are the moſt grateful offering we can preſent.

(The Indian to whom Ataliba gave his ſword, ruſhes upon the ſtage almoſt breathleſs.)

Indian. Victory is ours!

Ataliba. Meſſenger of Heaven!

Indian. (Laying the ſword at the king's feet.) Inca! receive back thy ſword; I have not diſgraced it!

Ataliba. Keep it, as a remembrance of this day.

Indian. Take back thy ſword, good king, and ſuffer me to forget this day. I had deſerted my poſt---I could not talk of it—could not ſhew the ſword to my grand-children.

Ataliba.

Ataliba. Is not the weapon dyed with the blood of our enemies ?—all former ftains are wafhed away. Now, give me the particulars of your victory.

Indian. Rolla's valour alone changed the fortune of the day, and fnatched the laurels from the heads of our conquerors. He was animated with more than mortal courage. When all was in diforder, and the enemy had maintained the purfuit till their fwords were weary with flaughter, Rolla threw himfelf into the midft of the affrighted multitude, with eyes darting forth lightning. He menaced, he intreated, he perfuaded---one moment his voice was like the rolling of the awful thunder, the next like the foothing ftrain of the dying fwan—one moment he turned his fword againft thofe who fled, the next againft his own breaft. At length he fucceeded in ftopping the fugitives, affembled a fmall but determined party around him, feized the ftandard of the Incas, and once more pufhed forwards. The Spaniards, confidering themfelves as fecure of the victory, had already begun to plunder the flain; and had thus broken their clofe ranks. Rolla's arm, aided by the gods, foon decided the conteft, and in a few moments every thing affumed a new afpect :---the enemy fell without refiftance, or fled uttering dreadful fhrieks, while we remained mafters of the field of battle. Stop ! cried Rolla —Victory ! exclaimed the army with loud fhouts of tranfport ; while I haftened hither with the joyful tidings.

Ataliba. Where is this hero ?---the Saviour of his country !---where is Rolla ?

Indian. On his way hither.

Ataliba. Now do I feel, indeed, that even kings are poor !

SCENE VIII.—ROLLA *enters, bearing the ftandard of the Incas, ornamented with the figure of the Sun.---He is accompanied by a large train of the foldiers and the people.* ATALIBA *advances to meet him, he kneels and lays the ftandard at the king's feet.*

Rolla. Hail, conqueror !
Ataliba. (*Embracing him)* My friend !---my protector !

F 2   *The*

The People. Long live Rolla!!!

Ataliba. *(Taking from his own neck a golden chain to which a diamond sun is suspended, and hanging it round Rolla's)* In the name of my people, whose saviour thou hast this day proved, I present thee with this testimony of our gratitude. The tears which have fallen upon it will best speak the feelings of thy king.

Rolla. *(Rising up)* I was only the instrument of the gods.

Old Man. Ah! how haplefs is the lot of the poor blind old man, that he can only listen to the hero!

Ataliba. Let us hasten to the women who anxiously expect us.

Rolla. Where is Alonzo?

Ataliba. *(Mournfully)* With the gods.

Rolla. Oh, miserable that I am!

An Indian. He fell in battle.

Another. He was taken prisoner.

The First. I myself saw him fall.

The Second. I saw him dragged away.

Rolla. Poor Cora!

Ataliba. Dearly-purchased victory!

First Indian. He fell; but is alive still.

Second Indian. I heard him at a distance calling for help.

Rolla. And Rolla did not hear his brother's voice!

Ataliba. The gods required a sacrifice!---thy friend is lost---thy native country saved!---the shouts of the people will stifle the sounds of our lamentations. But come, let us hasten to the women who are become widows!---to the children who are become orphans!---To dry the tears of his subjects is one of the most sacred duties of a sovereign.

Rolla. And must I see Cora, without Alonzo!

[*Exeunt omnes.*

END OF THE SECOND ACT.

ACT III.

SCENE I.----*An open Space in a Forest---several Women, and Children disposed in different Groups.*

CORA *sits under a Tree; with her Child lying by her, upon a Bed of Moss.*

CORA.

STILL dost thou sleep, lovely infant ? Wilt thou not yet unclose those blue eyes, that, in contemplating them, thy anxious mother may fancy she beholds thy father's !--- Ah, where are now thy father's blue eyes ?---Do they still shine ?---does he still live ?

One of the Women. (*Speaking to another, who stands upon a hill, at a little distance*) Xuliqua ! do you see nothing ?

Xuliqua. (*Answering from the hill*) A few moments since, I saw a thick cloud of dust ; but it is now dispersed.

Another Woman. The battle must soon be decided.

A Third. As I stood upon the hill, I heard a clashing of spears.

A Fourth. I could distinguish a hollow clangor.

The First. That proceeded from the shields of our people.

The Third. We must all have heard the Spaniards' fire arms.

The Second. The gods protect our husbands !

Cora.

Cora. (*Aside---raiſing her hands towards heaven*) God protect Alonzo!

Firſt Woman. Xuliqua! do you ſee nothing?

Xuliqua. (*Still ſpeaking from the hill*) The ſun blinds me.

Firſt Woman. Our Father looks down upon us with ſmiles---the children of the Sun will conquer.

Cora. (*To her child.*) Ah, my poor boy!---a gnat has ſtung him. (*She breaks off a little bough from the tree, with which ſhe fans him*) Oh, Alonzo! thy wife torments herſelf here about the ſting of a gnat; while perhaps an arrow may have pierced thee to the heart!

* *Firſt Woman.* Xuliqua! do you ſee nothing?

Xuliqua. I ſee a man running---and at a ſtill greater diſtance, I ſee another. They ſeem both to be haſtening hither.

The Women. Ye good gods!---tidings of our huſbands! tidings of our huſbands!

Xuliqua. (*Deſcending from the hill*) The firſt had diſappeared from my ſight among the trees---he will be here immediately.

Cora. My heart will ſpring through my boſom.

One of the Women. Here he is!---Well, what news?--- ſpeak quickly! joy or ſorrow? (*Speaking to a Peruvian, who enters panting for breath.*)

Peruvian. We are defeated! ſave yourſelves! (*The Women ſhriek, Cora ſinks down by her child*) Save yourſelves!---all is loſt! The king is wounded!---perhaps already dead!

The Women. (*All together*) Oh, day of miſery!

Cora. (*In a faint voice*) And Alonzo?

Peruvian. I have not ſeen him.

The Women. Whither ſhall we run?

Peruvian. Farther into the foreſt.

The Women. Haſten, ſiſters!---collect every thing together! away! away!

Cora. I cannot go! (*The Women are about to depart as another Peruvian enters*)

Second Peruvian. Whither ſo faſt? there is ſtill hope.

The Women. Hope!---how?---what?

Second Peruvian. Rolla has rallied the fugitives---he

he raves, and rushes upon the enemy like a wounded
lion.

The Women. Rolla!---the favourite of the gods!

Cora. And Alonzo?

Second Peruvian. I have not seen him.

The Women. Is the king really wounded?

Second Peruvian. He was borne wounded from the
field of battle.

The Women. Why was he not brought hither?

Second Peruvian. I saw him stagger---saw his sacred
blood flow from the wound.

A Woman. (*Falling on her knees*) Pray, sisters! pray
for our good king's life!

All. (*Kneeling*) Ye gods, protect the first-born of the
Sun!

Cora. (*Faintly, as she falls upon her knees*) Thou only
God! restore me my Alonzo!---My child, clasp thy little
hands together---Pray for thy father and thy country!

A Third Peruvian. (*Eagerly as he enters*) Rejoice!
rejoice!---we are victorious!

The Women. (*Springing up*) Oh, welcome! welcome!
thou messenger of joy! (*They all surround him, and almost
stifle him with their caresses.*)

Third Peruvian. Pray, release me! I cannot tell you
more!

The Women. Is the king alive?

Third Peruvian. Yes, yes, he is!

The Women. Speak!---tell us all!

Third Peruvian. It was Rolla gained the victory.

The Women. Blessings upon the head of Rolla!

Cora. And Alonzo?

Third Peruvian. I have not seen him.

The Women. Let us depart!---let us hasten to our
husbands and brothers!

Third Peruvian. Stay, they will be here immediately.

The Women. They come! they come!

Third Peruvian. They followed close after me.

One of the Women. Sisters, let us gather boughs and
twine them into wreaths, to crown the conquerors.

All. Wreaths! wreaths to crown the conquerors!---
(*They gather boughs, and begin to twine them together.*)

Cora.

Cora. Not one of them has feen him!---O, my child!
haft thou ftill a father living! (*A march is heard at a
diflance.*)

One of the Women. Ha! they come! Stand afide, my
fifters, let us make way for the heroes---let us view them
as they march along in triumph; and let us raife our
children in our arms, that they may unite their little voices
with ours to hail them victors. (*As the mufic approaches
nearer, the women join in a fhout of tranfport*) Hail to the
children of the Sun!---Bleffings on Rolla, the conqueror!
Bleffings on Ataliba, our father and our king, whom
Rolla's arm hath faved!

SCENE II.---*Enter the* KING *and* ROLLA, *followed by
a long train of Soldiers. The Women mix among them,
with joyful acclamations. and place the wreaths on the
heads of* ATALIBA *and* ROLLA.

Ataliba. I thank you, my children.

Several of the Women. You are wounded, good king?
Where is the wound?---We have a healing balfam preffed
from herbs of wonderous virtue.

Ataliba. I thank you; but the wound is flight, and
I have found the victory a fovereign balfam.

Cora. (*With her child in her arms, has been fearching
for Alonzo among the Soldiers, and at length comes up de-
fpairingly to Rolla, who flands wrapt in mournful mufing*)
Where is Alonzo?---(*Rolla turns away in filence; Cora
fals at the king's feet*) Give me back my hufband!---
give back a father to this child!

Ataliba. (*Endeavouring to conceal his uneafinefs*) Is
not Alonzo yet returned?

Cora. You expect his return, then?

Ataliba. (*Raifing her up*) With the utmoft anxiety.

Cora. He is not dead?

Ataliba. The gods, I truft, will hear my prayers!

Cora. He is not dead?

Ataliba. He lives in my heart.

Cora. Oh, king!---you torture me!---away with thefe
equivocal expreffions!---crufh me with a fingle blow at
once!---

once!—Tell me that I am a widow!—that this child is an orphan!

Ataliba. Why, deareft Cora, would you, by gloomy anticipation, diminifh the little hope that remains to us?

Cora. Little!—yet ftill *hope!*---What am I to underftand from this?---Speak, Rolla!---you are a friend to truth.

Rolla. Alonzo is miffing.

Cora. Miffing!---You do not deal plainly with me---you evade the queftion!---Oh keep not your lightning thus playing round me at a diftance; let it defcend directly upon my head!---fay at once, that he is dead!

Rolla. Would you wifh me to utter a falfhood?

Cora. The gods be praifed, if it be indeed, a falfhood!—But has not one among you fufficient compaffion to relieve me from this inexpreffible torment!---Lift up thy little hands, poor child; perhaps thy infant cries may prove more eloquent than thy mother's agonies!

Rolla. Alonzo is taken prifoner.

Cora. Prifoner! and by the Spaniards!---Oh, God! then his death is certain!

Ataliba. Let us hope better. I will immediately fend a herald to Pizarro, with the offer of a large fum of money for his ranfom.

Cora. His ranfom!---Where are my jewels? (*She gives him a cafket*) Give thefe to the herald.

Ataliba. Will not Cora allow me the fatisfaction of purchafing the life of my friend?

Cora. Is a ranfom wanted for my hufband, and can I think of retaining any thing for myfelf, except the cloaths I wear?

Several of the women. (*After whifpering among themfelves bring each a cafket, which they prefent to Cora*) Here, Cora, accept thefe ornaments which we have been anxious to preferve.---Accept them, we entreat!---they are given with fincere good-will.

Cora. (*Embracing them*) Oh, my friends!

Ataliba. (*Raifing his eyes towards heaven*) God, I thank thee, for making me ruler over fuch a people!

Cora. Thanks fhall be the firft found this child is taught to utter. Take thefe jewels, Ataliba, take them, and difpatch the herald.

G

Ataliba.

Ataliba. Without delay. (*He gives the collected orna-ments to his train*).

Cora. I will accompany the herald myself; and those whom the fight of gold cannot allure, may be moved by my tears.

Ataliba. No, Cora, this muft not be!---you would only expofe both yourfelf and Alonzo to more imminent danger. Wait for the herald's return.

Cora. Teach me to endure life till that hour!

Ataliba. Do not forget the mother in the wife. Would you entruft your infant to ftrange hands, or take him with you, to become a prey to the barbarous Spaniards? Think, alfo, what would be the fate of your charms among fuch monfters?---Believe me, that by fo rafh a ftep, you would hazard your own life, your honour, and the life of your child, while, inftead of faving Alonzo, the fight of you would only rivet his chains more firmly. In one word, Cora, you *muft* remain here; you are a mother---that muft not be forgotten.

Cora. (*Looking anxioufly at her child*)   It fhall not be forgotten!

Ataliba. I go to offer to the gods, my thanks for our victory, and my prayers for Alonzo's fafety.

Cora. You go!---Firft, give me your royal word, that Alonzo fhall return this evening.

Ataliba. Can I do fo?

Cora. Can you *not* do it!---Then ftill his death is pof-fible?---Oh! why fo quiet poor orphan?---cry, cry, aloud! Require your father of this man!---for this man he died!

Ataliba. You rend my heart!---will it be a lighter affliction to me, than to yourfelf, fhould Alonzo not re-turn, fhall not I then fuftain an irreparable lofs?---The wife may again find an affectionate hufband; but where fhall the king find fuch another friend? (*Exeunt Ataliba, and his train, with the women and children*).

SCENE III.----*Manent.* CORA *and* ROLLA.

Cora. Miferable confolation!---Poor child, what will become of thee!

Rolla.

Rolla. Do not abandon thyself to despair, Cora; trust in the gods.

Cora. They have forsaken me.

Rolla. They created friendship as a balm for every wound.

Cora. It cannot heal mine.

Rolla. They planted the flowers of hope in the soil of affliction.

Cora. To me they are all withered.

Rolla. Despair disturbs thy senses; anguish makes thee ungrateful. What the gods miraculously gave thee, by a miracle may be restored.

Cora. And if not—if Alonzo——ah, I cannot speak it!

Rolla. Can thy child be fatherless, while Rolla lives?

Cora. Can Rolla also supply the place of his mother?—or does he suppose, that I can survive the loss of Alonzo?

Rolla. For the sake of this child.

Cora. Shall my child draw blood from this tortured breast?—Shall he bathe only in his mother's tears?

Rolla. The lenient hand of time—the king's friendship—my love—

Cora. Away with your friendship—your love!—Would you give a handful of grass to the countryman whose germinating seeds have been destroyed by hail, and hope thus to repair his loss?

Rolla. Refuse not to hearken to Alonzo's friend, at least, even if resolved not to listen to your own.

Cora. Alonzo's friend!—Tell me, who was not his friend?

Rolla. His last words before the battle——

Cora. His last words!—Oh, speak! what were they?

Rolla. He charged me with two important commissions—to carry his blessing to his son,—and a wish to you.

Cora. A wish!—his last wish!—Instantly let me hear it!

Rolla. "If I fall," said he, and pressed my hand, while his whole frame trembled, "then be Cora thy wife!"

Cora. Thy wife!

Rolla. I gave him my word; and we parted.

Cora. Ha!—a horrible light breaks in upon me! Oh, Alonzo! thou hast fallen a sacrifice to thy unsuspecting heart

heart!—Hadſt thou been ſilent, inſtead of making theſe
wretched charms a fatal inheritance————

Rolla.   Oh, God! what a hateful ſuſpicion has ſeized
your mind!

Cora.   It is too clear!—Yes; you placed him in a ſi-
tuation where it was impoſſible to avoid death!—his valour made him an eaſy dupe to your artifice—he flew—
he ruſhed among the ſwords of the enemy—you looked
on, at a diſtance, and ſmiled!

Rolla.   (*In the utmoſt aſtoniſhment*)   Cora!

Cora.   Or was it only that you ſaw him in danger,
when it was in your power to ſave him;—but the recol-
lection of his legacy croſſed your mind—you turned away,
and he fell?

Rolla.   Oh, glorious Sun! why have I lived to ſee this
day?

Cora.   No!—no!—thou didſt not murder him!—the
wretched widow has no reaſon to complain of thee!—
the hand thou offereſt her is not ſtained with her huſband's blood!—thou wert only a calm ſpectator of his
death!

Rolla.   This is too much!

Cora.   And this laſt wiſh!—Ah! who knows whether
it ever paſſed Alonzo's lips! the dead are ever courteous—

Rolla.   Cora, take my ſword, and diſpatch me at once!

Cora.   No: live for the ſake of love!—a love, the
bloſſoms of which ſhoot from the grave of thy departed
friend?—But hear me, firſt,—liſten to my ſolemn oath, as
thou didſt to Alonzo's laſt wiſh?—Sooner ſhall my ſon im-
bibe poiſon from this breaſt, than he ſhall call thee father!
than I will call thee huſband!

Rolla.   Then call me, your friend—your protector.

Cora.   Away!—I know no other protector but God!
—I will haſten inſtantly to the field of battle,—with
this child in my arms, examine every mangled corpſe I
find on that fatal ſpot, to ſee if I cannot diſcern on the
countenance, though disfigured by death, that ſweet ſmile
which uſed to animate my huſband's features—I will call
on the name of Alonzo, with fearful ſhrieks, till my veins
burſt in my boſom; that if one ſpark of life yet remain but
half extinguiſhed, he may hear my voice, uncloſe his eyes,

and

and bless me with a last look. But if I do not find him,—
then, my son, we will throw ourselves into the enemy's
arms ;—the Spaniards are also men, and thy infant-smiles
will open me a path through a thousand swords. Who
will thrust back a wife that seeks her husband? who spurn
an innocent child that cries for his father? Come, sweet
boy, we shall be safe any where !—a mother with a child
at her breast, carries a passport, signed by the hand of nature herself, which will secure her a hospitable reception in
every part of the world.—Come, let us seek thy father!
(*She rushes out.*)

SCENE IV.—ROLLA *alone.*

(*He stands for some time motionless, with his eyes gloomily
fixed upon the earth, till at length overpowered by his feelings, he exclaims in a tone of anguish*) This to me ! (*He
sinks again into deep musing, his eyes roll wildly, till at
length he says with manly resolution*) I will compel her to
esteem me ! [*Exit.*

SCENE V.---PIZARRO's *tent in the Spanish camp.*

PIZARRO *alone, walking backwards and forwards in gloomy
agitation.*

Fortune ! thou jilt ! thy delight is to play the wanton
with boys---man's arm is too rough for thee !---He who
has only down upon his chin, whose cheeks are still un-
furrowed, is flattered and caressed by thee, while from
him, upon whose manly brow prudence sits enthroned,
thou turnest aside with disdain, nor wilt bestow upon him
one favourable glance. Thou meretricious monster ! roll
on thy wheel ! drive it exultingly over my mangled corpse!
yet first grant me vengeance !---vengeance upon Alonzo !
---Smile upon me but once more, and be that smile the
signal for Alonzo's fall.

SCENE

SCENE VI.---*Enter* ELVIRA.

Pizarro. Who comes there ?---who has dared to grant you admittance ? Where is my guard ?

Elvira. Your guard has done all that could be expected from even the moft vigilant. " *Who is there ?"* —— " *'Tis I, Elvira."*—" *Go back"*—" *For what reafon"*— " *Pizarro chufes to be alone, and has given the ftrifteft prohibition'*—Then, a gentle glance from me glided from his briftly hair above, to his briftly beard below—the halberd was lowered—and—here I am.

Pizarro. What do you want ?

Elvira. To fee how a hero bears misfortune.

Pizarro. Did you not, this day, fee me in the midft of my fcattered troops, when with my own hands I thruft the daftards back into the fight ?—Did you not fee me, afterwards at the head of my defeated army,—when, amid thoufands who appeared wholly abafhed and difmayed—my firmnefs alone was unfubdued ?—you know then, that I can defy misfortune.

Elvira. I faw you, it is true, in both thofe fituations ; but to know a hero thoroughly, he muft alfo be feen, in private, in his tent. Many a one will difplay great magnanimity before thoufands, who cannot preferve like fortitude when alone. Many a one, amid the filence and folitude of night, will tremble at a phantom of his own creation, who in the face of an army would encounter death with undaunted refolution.

Pizarro. Well, then, you now fee me here. Are my features clouded with unmanly forrow :—or do you hear me uttering idle lamentations ?

Elvira. Lamentations !—from Pizarro !—Lamentations are only for priefts and women. But you gnafh your teeth, and even that is beneath you.

Pizarro. Would you have me give a ball, and folicit your hand to open it, becaufe the fword of the enemy is glutted with the braveft blood in our army.

Elvira. No, I would have you cold and filent as the night, when the ftorm has fpent its fury—cold and filent as the grave on the eve of the refurrection. Then when the

the morning dawns, the hero will emerge again with re-
novated powers, and shine forth with added splendour irra-
diated by a new sun.

Pizarro. Oh! why were not all my men, on this day,
women like Elvira!

Elvira. Then had my hand even now crowned you
king of Quito. Yet, reflect, that we are still resting upon
the same shore---the crown which this morning seemed
within your grasp yet hovers before your eyes ; arm yourself then with new courage, spring forward, and seize it
ere it vanish.

Pizarro. Oh, Elvira! my hopes are faint, as long as
this Alonzo, this scourge of my life, leads on the enemy.

Elvira. Ah! I had forgotten to inform you, that
Alonzo is your prisoner.

Pizarro. How?

Elvira. Even now he has been dragged in triumph
through the camp, by some of our soldiers.

Pizarro. (*Embracing her*) Elvira what glorious tidings do you communicate !---Alonzo my prisoner !---Oh!
then, I am conqueror ! --I have defeated the enemy !

Elvira. My curiosity is extremely excited by these
transports.---There must surely be something extraordinary in a man of whom Pizarro stands so much in awe,
---I am impatient to see him.

Pizarro. Where is he ?---Guards ! (*Enter one of the
guards*) Let the Spanish prisoner be immediately brought
hither ! (*Exit the guard*)

Elvira. What will you do with him ?

Pizarro. He shall die !---die in torments, protracted to
the utmost extent that nature can endure.

Elvira. Shame on thee !---think what will then be
said by posterity ?---that Pizarro could not conquer, till
Alonzo was murdered.

Pizarro. No matter !

Elvira. What a sentiment to proceed from your
mouth. Still, Pizarro, let me conjure you to act nobly,
if not for his sake, at least for your own.

Pizarro. And what would you call acting nobly?

Elvira. Give Alonzo a sword, and challenge him to
single combat.

Pizarro. He has abjured his native country, perhaps
also

alfo his God ;---and fhall a traitor be honoured with a hero's death ?

Elvira. Follow thy own pleafure ;---but mark me ! ---If he be murdered, Elvira is loft to thee for ever.

Pizarro. What can excite this intereft for a ftranger ? ---What is he to you ?

Elvira. He is nothing to me, but *your* fame, every thing. Do you fuppofe it is you I love?—no, it is your fame.

Pizarro. Fame is not the object to which I afpire ! My heart pants for revenge ;---I have fworn that it fhall be fatisfied; and I am a Spaniard.

SCENE VII.—ALONZO *is brought in chained.* ELVIRA *obferves him for fome moments with a mixture of curiofity and admiration:*

Pizarro. Welcome, Don Alonzo de Molina !---we have not met for a long time.

Alonzo. And, even now, meet again too foon.

Pizarro. You are grown fat, fince I faw you laft.

Alonzo. Yet I have not fed upon blood and rapine.

Pizarro. I am informed, too, that you are married !--- perhaps already a father ?

Alonzo. Would you be mortified to hear that it is no longer poffible to murder the child in his mother's womb ?

Pizarro. (*His eyes flafhing with rage*) Prefumptuous boy !

Elvira. You are rightly anfwered; why did you in- fult him ?

Pizarro. Who has appointed you his advocate !

Elvira. To infult the unfortunate is contemptible.

Pizarro. Hence ! or dread my anger !

Elvira. I will not leave you.

Pizarro. Will you compel me to employ force ?

Elvira. (*Drawing out a dagger*) Force !

Alonzo. Noble youth, who are you ?---I am a ftranger to your perfon.

Elvira. If I be really noble, of what importance is my name ?

Alonzo.

Alonzo. Spare yourfelf!—any endeavour to defend me is feeking to rob a tyger of his prey.

Pizarro. Which tyger is called *juftice.*

Alonzo. What a facred name is profaned by thy lips!

Pizarro. Thou art a traitor to thy native country.

Alonzo. Was I born among robbers?

Pizarro. Thou art an apoftate from thy God and thy religion.

Alonzo. 'Tis falfe.

Pizarro. Thy wife is a heathen.

Alonzo. The Almighty knows, and judges, *all* hearts.

Pizarro. And pays them according to their deferts.

Alonzo. In another world.

Pizarro. Thy moments are numbered; defend thyfelf if it be poffible.

Alonzo. Where are my judges?

Pizarro. Doft thou afk that?

Alonzo. Are you then defpot here?

Pizarro. Would you appeal to the affembled Council of War?

Alonzo. If Las-Cafas be among you—if not—that trouble may as well be fpared.

Pizarro. Rafhnefs always feeks to fhelter itfelf under the follies of others!

Alonzo. Las-Cafas a fool?—Then, let me be fpared any inftruction in your wifdom! and the Almighty grant that I may live and die in the follies of Las-Cafas!

Pizarro. The accomplifhment of that wifh may be nearer than you imagine.

Alonzo. Do you expect to terrify me?

Pizarro. And fuppofing Las-Cafas were in my place; what would you urge to him?

Alonzo. I would take him by the hand, lead him through the verdant and flourifhing fields of Quito, point out where the plough-fhare has rendered fertile a barren foil, and where a luxuriant crop promifes a rich recompenfe to our toils—then tell him—" *this is my work!*" I would fhew him how content fmiles upon every countenance, while mild and gentle inftitutes fuperfede barbarous laws, and tell him, " *this is my work!*" Shew him, how, already, many a hand, many an eye, is raifed in pure de-

H   votion

votion to the only true God; and tell him, " *this is my work !*"—Oh! then would Las-Cafas clafp me in his arms, while tears of plealing fadnefs would drop bleffings upon my head !—'Tis by deeds like thefe, that man becomes enabled to fmile defiance upon death.

Pizarro. You remain what you have always been—an enthufiaft.

Alonzo. Could I renounce fuch enthufiafm, I fhould indeed deferve to be called—Pizarro's friend.

Pizarro. Well, fmile defiance upon death ; for know that they who fit in council here, are not women, but men.

Alonzo. I know the manlinefs of which you boaft, and am refigned to my fate.

Pizarro. 'Tis well—for your remaining hours of life are few. Prepare for death.

Alonzo. I am prepared.

Pizarro. Has this fublime enthufiafm entirely fuppreffed all folicitude for your wife and child.

Alonzo. There is a God, on whom I rely for their protection.

Pizarro. I congratulate thee upon thy haughty refolution.—Go then, addrefs thyfelf to God, for the firft ray of to-morrow's fun, is the harbinger of thy death.

Alonzo. Thy vengeance requires hafte---I thank thee *(Going.)*

Elvira. Stay, Alonzo !—I tell thee, Pizarro, he fhall not die.

Pizarro. Are you befide yourfelf?

Elvira. It is not exalted virtue,—it is not magnanimity I require of thee,—I afk merely what is due to thy own honour. Set him at liberty, give him a fword, and challenge him to fingle combat. Act otherwife, and you become the object of my fettled fcorn.

Pizarro. Set him at liberty, that he may again dye his hands in the blood of his brethren !

Alonzo. Robbers are not my brethren.

Pizarro. Do you hear him ?—hence, Alonzo !—you know your fentence.

Alonzo. I know, and defpife it.—For thee, fweet youth, *(To Elvira)* accept my thanks—but in this camp thou doft not feem in thy proper fphere—go among the favages,

as

as they are called; thou wilt find in them companions more congenial to thy heart.

[*Exit.*

SCENE VII.—Pizarro *and* Elvira.

Pizarro. Now, revile me, Madam, if you pleafe, and pour oil upon the flame of my revenge. This proud calmnefs befpeaks the pupil of Las-Cafas.

Elvira. I admire this Alonzo.

Pizarro. Within a few hours that tone will be changed, and you may fay with a tender figh, I *did* admire this Alonzo.

Elvira. You, really, are refolved upon his death?

Pizarro. 'Tis as certain as that the fun fhall rife.

Elvira. And the manner?—

Pizarro. Remains to be confidered. I muft calculate how much torture can be compreffed into the fhort fpace of an hour.

Elvira. I could name a fpecies of torture, which inflicts the fevereft anguifh upon the fufferer, while at the fame time it gives exalted pleafure to the tormentor.

Pizarro. Name it.

Elvira. 'Tis to call forth upon the cheeks of the villain, the blufh of fhame at the confcioufnefs of villany detected.

Pizarro. I do not underftand you.

Elvira. Pardon him!

Pizarro. That again?

Elvira. And a thoufand times over. Pizarro, I deferve thy bleffing for feeking to avert from thee the curfes of pofterity. In the records of hiftory it will hereafter appear that you landed in a foreign hemifphere with only a handful of troops, and defeated the fovereign of a powerful kingdom;—then will the reader obferve, " *this man was* BRAVE !"—If it be farther related, that you pardoned a haughty enemy in chains; then will he exclaim with admiration, " *this man was* GREAT ! •

Pizarro. And my mouldering bones will then rattle with tranfport in my coffin?

H 2

Elvira.

Elvira. Pofthumous fame may be deemed a bubble; and the hero who runs after it, a child; yet this toy too often transforms the man into the demi-god.

Pizarro. But fuppofe I only fatisfy a juft revenge?—What will then be faid?

Elvira. " *He thruft a dagger into the heart of an enemy in chains;—he was not above the common level of mankind.*"

Pizarro. (*With a fmile of contempt*) Hercules fqueezed to death the giant Antæus, and Marfyas was flayed by Apollo.

Elvira. Does Alonzo play the flute better than you?—would you therefore flay him?

Pizarro. Enough, Elvira, your eloquence is thrown away.

Elvira. You are right,—who would attempt to plant cedars in a moor. But let us now take another view of the matter. Fame, whether acquired during our life, or only granted by pofterity, is perhaps fcarcely worth a reafonable man's attention;—'tis a vapour, a flame, which can neither feed nor warm us. But difregard not at leaft your own advantage—and, how fay you, if by a little magnanimity, which will coft you nothing, an important object may be obtained?

Pizarro. Speak more plainly!

Elvira. Alonzo muft, and will, continue to fhew himfelf the difciple of Las-Cafas; but whether through an heroic death, by which we cannot be gainers, or by a folly which will prove highly advantageous to us, refts entirely with you.

Pizarro. How fo?

Elvira. An enthufiaft muft be caught by phantoms of his own creation. That ideal being to which mankind has given the name of exalted virtue, is his idol. Go, then, fay to him, Alonzo, you have injured me, but I pardon you freely, you are at liberty. What follows?—the boy finks upon your bofom, and out of pure gratitude betrays the throne of Quito into your hands.

Pizarro. Do you fuppofe fo?—I doubt it much.

Elvira. Is it, that the means propofed are too hard to you?—then may I be your affiftant. Where does love reign fo abfolute as in the heart of the enthufiaft?—over whom has he equal power, either to lead him into good, or to

draw

draw him aside into evil? I am young, I have charms, am not deftitute of underftanding, and know well how to mould the humours of man to my own purpofes. You muft be fenfible, Pizarro, that while thoufands obey you as a hero, you obey me as a woman.

Pizarro. I obey you?—

Elvira. Say not a word—the time is precious. I will go to Alonzo—as a youth I have acquired an intereft in his heart, and when I ftand before him as a woman, when he prefs my hand within his, when my eyes are fixed upon him in tender entreaty, when the language of virtue flows from my lips, think you, he can refufe me any thing?

Pizarro. Your vanity is amufing.

Elvira. Thank me for the hint, ere I repent of having given it.

Pizarro. I leave you to immediate, perhaps to perpetual repentance, for my refolution is fixed.

Elvira. That Alonzo fhall die?—

Pizarro. That he fhall die.

Elvira. Though, at the fame moment, you lofe Elvira for ever?

Pizarro. Though I lofe her for ever.

Elvira. And fhe fhould feek refuge with a nobler enemy,—fhould join with Alonzo in labouring to promote the Peruvians' happinefs.

Pizarro. To that, I can oppofe chains and bonds.

Elvira. Chains and bonds to a woman! to one who, without having imbibed the mild precepts of Las-Cafas, has yet learned to defpife death.

Pizarro. Even the latter may be your lot.

Elvira. Pizarro, you no longer love me.

Pizarro. If you hope to transform a General into a whining Shepherd; you will find yourfelf miftaken.

Elvira. Ungrateful man!—Have you forgotten that you alone were the caufe of my quitting my parents and native country? that for your fake I refolved to defy danger, and either bury myfelf in your arms, or in the bofom of the ocean.

Pizarro. Have I not amply repaid this mighty attachment? Are not you the fharer of my power, my joys?

Elvira. Recollect, that I equally fhare your peril.— On this dreadful day, amid the throng of battle, who remained

mained firmly and conftantly at your fide?—who prefented as a fhield to you, a breaft unaccuftomed to the fteely armour by which your's is defended?

Pizarro. Deareft Elvira, while in valour you are a man, in love you are a perfect woman. 'My whole heart, and half my booty, by right, are your's.

Elvira. Half your booty?—then I claim Alonzo as my prifoner.

Pizarro. Excufe me!—I referve the divifion to myfelf.

Elvira. Can you refufe, when I entreat, when I moiften your cheek with my tears?

Pizarro. Yes, even then.---(*After a paufe*) Elvira, what am I to think of this?---Are you captivated by the boy's fmooth face?

Elvira. No, I love you ftill; but I wifh to fee you worthy of my love. In battle, chance may fnatch the victory out of your hands, but in a conteft with yourfelf, victory is always in your own power, and thefe are the moft glorious of all triumphs, 'tis then that you truly appear a hero---and none but a hero can Elvira love.

Pizarro. You entreat in vain.---And take heed, Elvira, left this anxiety for the fate of a ftranger, fhould excite fufpicions in my breaft.---You know the Spanifh character---you know me.

Elvira. Yes, I do know thee!---I know thee to be jealous of female favour, jealous alfo of fame. Thou wilt not, by blafting the latter, render thyfelf unworthy of the former, and tear afunder the only bond which unites Elvira's heart to thine.

Pizarro. Every word you utter, confirms Alonzo's fentence.

Elvira. Then, our eternal feparation is fealed!---Go and whet thy fword for the neck of a prifoner, whofe chains are not confidered as a fufficient fecurity for thy precious life. Gladly has Elvira wiped away the blood and duft from the forehead of her hero after a battle, but never defiled her hands with the duft of flight, or the blood of affaffination. The arm which fhall be raifed againft a defencelefs enemy, never more fhall encircle a woman whofe foul is noble!—The lips which could unite mockery with a fentence of death, never fhall prefs mine!—I know well that revenge may be fweet and grateful to the heart,—but no
longer

longer than while the enemy is armed in defiance againſt us;—if he fall, vengeance falls with him.—He who feels otherwiſe, I pity—he who acts otherwiſe, I deſpiſe.

Pizarro. (*After a pauſe, looking at her with a contemptuous ſmile*) Thou art a woman!

[*Exit.*

SCENE IX.—ELVIRA *alone.*

A woman! knoweſt thou that,—and doſt thou not tremble?—Knoweſt thou, that as I love, ſo I can hate,—and doſt thou not tremble?—Yes, man of blood, whom neither the ſtrife of contending elements, nor the rage of a powerful enemy can terrify, thou ſhalt find thyſelf vulnerable to a woman who ſolemnly ſwears thy deſtruction. Alonzo ſhall live, and I will love him, not becauſe youth and beauty ſmile upon his blooming cheeks, but becauſe the idol which I worſhipped in Pizarro, inſtead of pure ore, has proved baſe metal—becauſe the temple, which appeared marble at a diſtance, has proved, on examination, merely varniſhed plaiſter.—Oh, Pizarro! Pizarro! I could even have pardoned the injury, if for the ſake of a throne thou hadſt proved faithleſs to thy promiſed love!—but thou haſt acted with meanneſs, and Elvira's heart is alienated for ever!—

[*Exit.*

END OF THE THIRD ACT.

ACT IV.

SCENE I.—*A Tent in the Spanish Camp. The Time is past Midnight.*

ALONZO *alone.*

DESPISE death!—Such was the maxim among the Greeks and Romans; heathens endowed with exalted wisdom. Shame, then, on thee, Christian, that thou canst tremble before him, since what to them was no more than conjecture. to thee is certainty,—that there is a better world!--Yet thou dost tremble!—Is it that the ardent sensibilities of youth revolt more keenly against an un-timely death, than the blunted feelings of age?—What is an untimely death?—Shall Alonzo calculate his life only by the years he has numbered?—Does he not possess Cora?—Cora!—ah, this is the rosy bond that chains me irresistibly to life! Wife and child!—one holds me back by the tears of love, the other by the smile of innocence!—Oh, Cassius, thou wert not a husband! Seneca, thou wert not a father!—The voice of nature cries LIVE, and my heart loudly echoes back the sound!—Can this wish be a re-proach to the man, and the hero?—Yet, Sovereign Dis-poser of my fate! though it were so, I must still wish to live!

SCENE II.—*Enter a* SOLDIER, *with two bottles of wine.*

Soldier. Here, Don Alonzo de Molina, be of good cheer, and drink.

Alonzo.

Alonzo. Who fent thee hither?
Soldier. I keep guard before your tent.
Alonzo. I thank your compaffion for this refrefhment.
Soldier. No thanks to me. 'Tis true, I am heartily grieved for your fituation; but 'tis not in my power to af- fift you,—for I am poor.
Alonzo. Who gave you this wine?
Soldier. One who can give much fweeter things than wine—(*whifpering*) Donna Elvira.
Alonzo. And who is Donna Elvira?
Soldier. Have you never heard of her?—She is our General's *friend.*
Alonzo. His friend?
Soldier. Yes, yes, his *friend*;—you underftand me.
Alonzo. And Elvira, you fay?—
Soldier. Sent you this wine.
Alonzo. Does fhe know me?
Soldier. Scarcely, I believe.
Alonzo. Go, and return her my thanks.
Soldier. Very well.
Alonzo. And take the wine with you.
Soldier. How?—won't you drink?
Alonzo. I have not drunk wine for feveral years.
Soldier. But a man in your fituation wants fupport, and thefe bottles would infpire you with a noble refolution.
Alonzo. My good friend, I pity the wretch who can- not meet death courageoufly, without fuch infpiration.
Soldier. But it confufes the fenfes, and deadens pain.
Alonzo. Leave me, I pray you. Death is not a phan- tom from which I would feek to conceal myfelf by hiding my face in my pillow. Drink the wine yourfelf;—the night is very cold, you will find it reviving.
Soldier. Certainly, I have no objection to that,—if you wifh it. To do you juftice it muft be owned, that you are a brave knight; only 'tis a fhame that you are become a heathen. If it were not finful, I could find in my heart to weep for you. [*Exit.*

SCENE III.—ALONZO *alone.*

Poor fellow! he knows not what he fays!—Thy bounties, oh God! are not confined to one country, one
I   religion!

religion !—Thou haft created the vine for the Spaniard,
and the plantain for the Peruvian !—Thy ftreams moiften,
alike the meadows at the foot of the Pyrenees, and
thofe bounded by the Cordilleras !—On our altars thou
haft erected the crofs as the fymbol of thy favour; but
thou fmileft equally upon the fun on the breaft of the
Incas !

SCENE IV.—*Enter* ELVIRA. *As fhe enters, fhe calls
to* ALONZO.

Elvira.   Don Alonzo !
Alonzo.   Who are you?—Come in.
Elvira.   (*Approaching him*) Do you not know me ?
Alonzo.   Yes, amiable youth, I remember you well.
You it was who ventured to expoftulate with the incenfed
Pizarro, when he pronounced fentence of death upon me.
Your form is indelibly impreffed upon my heart.
Elvira.   Live, Alonzo ! for, know that I love you.
Alonzo.   'Tis truly generous, yet not lefs dangerous to
fhew favour to the unfortunate.   At our former meeting,
you withheld from me your name :—but, oh, noble young
eagle, furrounded by vultures, fain would I know to whom
I am fo deeply indebted !
Elvira.   Can you not guefs ?
Alonzo.   How fhould that be poffible ?
Elvira.   Where has humanity erected a nobler tem-
ple, than in the breaft of woman ?—Who can venture to
defy tyrants with equal boldnefs, as woman ?
Alonzo.   Aftonifhment !—Is it a woman I behold ?
Perhaps Donna Elvira ?
Elvira.   The name, at leaft, feems not wholly unknown
to you ?—Yes, I am Elvira.
Alonzo.   Such a vifit !—at fuch an hour !—
Elvira.   One who haftens to fuccour the oppreffed, is
regardlefs of the hour.
Alonzo.   It is the laft of my life.
Elvira.   I tell you, no !
Alonzo.   Pizarro has fworn my death.
Elvira.   And I thy life.

Alonzo.

Alonzo. Accept my thanks—but I know how to die.

Elvira. For ever death and dying?—Are you one of those extraordinary beings who can sit calmly down upon the brink of the grave, and survey with complacency the gulf below?

Alonzo. What we cannot avoid, must be endured.

Elvira. Do you die willingly?

Alonzo. To answer that I do, were equally to deceive you and myself.

Elvira. Away, then!—instantly!

Alonzo. You can only joke?

Elvira. Then have I chosen an admirable time for sporting with a man.

Alonzo. These chains—my guards—

Elvira. To loosen chains, and blind the eyes of guards, is mere pastime to love.

Alonzo. To love!

Elvira. Call it what you will!—I, for my own part, am regardless whether or not I express my feelings according to scholastic rule. I saw you stand in chains before Pizarro; I heard you speak like an ancient Roman; and at that moment the chains glided from off your hands and fixed upon my heart. I felt it essential to my repose to save you: my soul is not formed to endure a tedious interval between the resolution and the action—I felt— and I have acted.

Alonzo. You come to save me?

Elvira. I come to save you, and to conjure you to save me!—to snatch me from this whirlpool where every struggle after fame is swallowed up in a torrent of blood! —to lead me from the path where avarice tramples the springing laurel beneath its feet!—I am not a woman cast in a common mould;—my love is not of that tame and sequestered kind which can be content to sit quietly down at the spinning-wheel, surrounded by my children and tell them pretty infant stories;—my heart thirsts for fame; and my lips must overflow with the noble actions performed by him I love. Look, my children, at this marble pillar;—it was erected to commemorate the illustrious deeds of your father. Hear ye those shouts of acclamation;—they are uttered in honour of your father. Stretch out your little hands to our reconciled foes;—your father has subdued them not less by magnanimity than

I 2

valour,

valour. Oh happy, thrice happy, the woman who can
thus addrefs thefe objects of her affection!—Of a love
like this our fex may juftly be proud ; and fuch is mine ;
—it is no common weaknefs. If on thefe terms, Alonzo,
I am fo fortunate as to pleafe you, be it your part to make
me forget the mifery of being born a woman—henceforth
we are united, and I fave you.

Alonzo. If I underftand you right, lovely woman, you
afk what is beyond my power to grant.—I am married.

Elvira. To a heathen.

Alonzo. Still fhe is my wife, and in every climate love
renders facred the bonds of wedlock.

Elvira. Does fhe return your affection with equal
tendernefs ?

Alonzo. Not merely with equal tendernefs. Donna
Elvira knows her fex, immeafurable alike in their love and
hatred.

Elvira. Yet you would make her a mournful widow.

Alonzo. Our fates are in the hand of God.

Elvira. The common refource of thofe who have not
fpirit enough to act for themfelves. Have you children ?

Alonzo. One pledge of the pureft love.

Elvira. Whom you would make an orphan.

Alonzo. Oh, my Fernando !

Elvira. Does it become the hero to lament, when he
ought to act with vigour?—Hear me!—If, indeed, you
are every thing to the heart of your wife ;—if fhe cannot
purchafe your fafety at too dear a rate ; fhe will joyfully
wave her claims upon you, and refign her hufband as a
recompenfe to his preferver.

Alonzo. That fhe would do moft willingly.

Elvira. Well then !—

Alonzo. Never!—A hafty death will foon break my
chains; and to avoid it, you would have me inflict on a
tender wife, forrows which only a lingering death could
terminate. With fuppreffed anguifh would fhe behold
me in your arms, while I fhould only fob upon your bofom. Lovers can facrifice any thing to their attachment,
but that attachment itfelf.—We are every thing to each
other.—I came into this country, to plunder it of its
wealth ; I have found here the choiceft of all earthly treafures, an affectionate wife ; and fhall I caft her from me,

                                                    to

to purchase a wretched exiſtence, which, without her, would be of no value? Oh, Cora! in your arms I have learnt what conſtitutes our only real happineſs; and never will I quit them but to reſt in the grave!—Leave me then, Signora,—leave me!—If on ſuch terms only, you can ſave my life; I am grateful for your intentions,—but farewel!

Elvira. I honour theſe ſentiments. Yet, ſuffer me to cheriſh the proud opinion, that had your heart been free, I had deſerved your love. Oh! I could almoſt envy your happy wife!—but away with the ignoble feeling!—haſten, Elvira, to ſtifle it by a diſintereſted action!—Come, then, Alonzo, take this dagger, and follow me; I will conduct you to the tent where Pizarro ſleeps, and you ſhall plunge it into his haughty and unfeeling heart. Terror will then ſpread its wings over the whole camp; while amid the confuſion raiſed by the firſt cry of murder, when the troops ſhall run hither and thither in wild aſtoniſhment, we will eſcape to your friends. There will I witneſs the tears of tranſport ſhed by your wife,—there will I hear the infant liſping of your child, and forget all my proud dreams. Come, follow me.

Alonzo. To murder a ſleeping man?

Elvira. Your bittereſt enemy.

Alonzo. I would not murder even the common enemy of all mankind, in his ſleep.

Elvira. I deteſt this Pizarro, becauſe he has been a traitor to me; and I deſpiſe him, becauſe he is mean enough to trample under foot a fallen enemy. Generoſity is due only to the generous!—deal by the villain as he would deal by others;—free the earth from a monſter who has been vomited forth from the Old World, to ſpread ruin and devaſtation in the New. Thy ſecond country will reward the deed with triumphant acclamations;—and honourable repoſe in the boſom of thy family will be the lot of thy future life. Haſte then, reſolve!

Alonzo. I am reſolved.

Elvira. To follow me.

Alonzo. No!—you muſt ſeek ſome other inſtrument to accompliſh your vengeance. There was a time when Pizarro loved me, when together we dared every honourable danger in the field of battle,—when I ſhared every meal that came to his table. An hundred times have I

ſlept

flept in peace by his fide! and fhall I murder him in his
fleep?

Elvira. Hath he not torn afunder every bond between
you?

Alonzo. The bond of his kindnefs to me can never be
deftroyed.

Elvira. Well, I will leave you a while. Solitude may
awaken reafon from her flumbers; and the terror of death
reftore you to your fenfes. Know that a large ranfom has
been offered for your freedom, which Pizarro has refufed;
and you have no other means of fafety remaining, but what
I propofe.

Alonzo. Then I muft die!

Elvira. Look toward the eaft—the ruddy ftreaks of
morning begin to appear, they announce the near approach
of your fate. The moments fly—but a few more are thine;
and the opportunity once loft, never can return. I leave
you to reflection. In a quarter of an hour I fhall return
to hear your final refolution.   [*Exit.*

SCENE V.—ALONZO *alone.*

Spare thyfelf fo fruitlefs an enquiry, it will be made in
vain!—Death may be a bitter medicine; but treachery is
a lufcious poifon!—Heaven guard and protect my wife
and child!—Heaven, and Rolla!—May they feek refuge
in the mountains where dwell innocence and peace! and
may my poor infant never know from what haplefs blood
he fprings.—Thou great Jehovah!—or Sun!—for the
name is indifferent to thee!—grant health and purity of
mind to thofe I leave behind me!—all elfe is idle vanity!—
Lo! there, the morning dawns over the hills; only one
hour more is mine; I will endeavour to deprive the fear
of death of its cuftomary tribute.—I will lay me down to
reft.—(*He lies down.*) Do thou, my unfullied confcience,
call fleep to the affiftance of thy friend!—my ftrength is
exhaufted; wearinefs preffes down my eye-lids!—Come,
gentle flumbers; prepare me for an acquaintance with
your more powerful brother! (*He falls afleep.*)

SCENE

SCENE VI.—*A* Soldier *on guard walks backwards and forwards before the entrance of* Alonzo's *Tent.*

Soldier.   Who's there?—anfwer quickly!—Who's there?

Rolla.   *(Behind the fcenes.)*   A prieft.

Soldier.   What would you here, Reverend Father?

Rolla.   *(Entering difguifed in the habit of a Monk)*—Friend, I pray you, inform me where I can find the Spaniſh prifoner, Alonzo?

Soldier.   He is in this tent.

Rolla.   Allow me to fpeak to him!

Soldier.   I dare not.

Rolla.   He is my friend.

Soldier.   Not, if he were your brother.

Rolla.   What is expeƈted to be his fate?

Soldier.   He dies at fun-rife.

Rolla.   Ha!—then I come at the proper moment.

Soldier.   To witnefs his death.

Rolla.   I muft fpeak with him.

Soldier.   Back—back—

Rolla.   Is he alone?

Soldier.   Yes.

Rolla.   I intreat you to let me fee him!

Soldier.   You afk in vain; our orders aie very ftriƈt.

Rolla.   *(Drawing out the diamond fun which he had received from the king)*   Look on thefe precious jewels.

Soldier.   And what of them?

Rolla.   They are your's; only let me fpeak with the prifoner.

Soldier.   Do you fuppofe me capable of being corrupted? know that I am an old Caftilian.

Rolla.   Take them, and perform a good aƈtion.

Soldier.   Back—back—I know my duty.

Rolla.   Are you married?

Soldier.   Yes.

Rolla.   Have you any children?

Soldier.   Four boys.

Rolla.   Where did you leave them?

Soldier.   *(In a foftened voice)*   At home, in my native country

Rolla.

Rolla. Do you love your wife and children?

Soldier. (*Much affected*) My God! Do I love them?

Rolla. Suppose you were to die in this foreign land?

Soldier. Then I should charge my comrades to carry them my last blessing.

Rolla. And if, when your comrades arrive at home, any one should be so inhuman as to refuse them admittance to your wife and children?

Soldier. How! What do you mean?

Rolla. Alonzo has a wife and child. That afflicted wife sent me hither to receive his last blessing for herself and her infant.

Soldier. Enter then.

Rolla. (*Advancing towards Alonzo.*) Oh sacred nature, thou art still true to thyself! Alonzo! where art thou! —Ha! there he lies asleep! (*Shakes him*) Alonzo!

Alonzo. (*Starting up*) Are you come for me so soon? —I am ready.

Rolla. Rouse thyself.

Alonzo. Ha!—What voice was that?

Rolla. 'Tis Rolla's voice.

Alonzo. Rolla!—am I indeed awake!—how came you hither?

Rolla. The present is not a time to waste in asking and answering questions. (*He takes off the Monk's habit*) For this disguise, I am indebted to the corpse of a priest who fell to-day in battle. Take it, and begone.

Alonzo. And you?—

Rolla. I will remain here in your place.

Alonzo. Never.

Rolla. No words, I intreat; but comply with my request.

Alonzo. And leave you to die for me!—rather twice endure the pangs of death myself!

Rolla. I shall not die. It is Alonzo's life that Pizarro seeks, not Rolla's. The utmost I have to fear, is a short imprisonment, from which your arm shall set me free.

Alonzo. How little do you know Pizarro's gloomy soul! When he shall find by what means he has been deprived of his prey, in the rage of disappointment, you will be instantly sacrificed to his revenge.

Rolla.

Rolla. No, no, a large ransom—

Alonzo. His thirst of vengeance even exceeds his avarice.

Rolla. And what if it should prove so?—I am alone in the world,—a single unconnected being, on whose life no other hangs—a solitary shrub standing in the midst of a sandy desert,—let it be cut down! who will feel its loss? —happy, only if it can thus become the means of warming one worthy heart. You, on the contrary, are a husband and a father,—the happiness or misery of a charming wife, and helpless infant, hang upon your life;—take the garment, therefore,—and away!

Alonzo. Would you make me the cowardly murderer of my friend?—would you save my life—only to embitter it with inexpressible torments?

Rolla. Never bestow a thought on me, but in Cora's arms. One tear mingled with the cup of joy, is all that I require. I have *lived* in the world to little purpose, do not deny me the consoling reflection, that at least I shall not *die* in vain.

Alonzo. Can a friend torture me thus?—My last hours were sufficiently painful without this.

Rolla. I cannot even bring you a farewel from a beloved wife; for she is insensible to every thing. She only recovers from one swoon, to fall into another.

Alonzo. Oh, my Cora!

Rolla. Her life is in danger, unless she see you speedily.

Alonzo. Her life!

Rolla. If you die, she dies; and your poor child is left an orphan.

Alonzo. Rolla will be his father.

Rolla. Do you suppose, that Rolla can survive the loss of Cora?

Alonzo. Grant me strength, Oh God, to support this conflict!

Rolla. And what do you expect to gain by your obduracy?—If you will not escape, neither will I. Here I am determined to remain, nor shall any power force me from you.—You shall be gratified with the pleasing spectacle of beholding Rolla fall by your side; then will Cora be left utterly forlorn.

K *Alonzo.*

Alonzo. Oh, Rolla! my feelings are nearly (
powered.

Rolla. A moment's paufe, and all is loft !—efc
and all may yet be well. We need not fear fent
being immediately paffed upon me. I will amufe Piz
with hopes of making important difcoveries.—I
endeavour to protract the time while you repair to
camp, collect a body of chofen young men, and at 1
burft like a ftorm upon our enemies, and lead back
friend in triumph. Haften, Alonzo, the day breaks,
not delay ; but fly to Cora's arms, fave her life, and
return to fave mine.

Alonzo. Rolla, whither would you drive me ?

Rolla. Do I require any thing difhonourable ?
throws the friar's garment over Alonzo) Conceal thy 1
and hold thy chains faft, that their clanking may not b
thee. There, go, and God be with thee !—remembe
kindly to Cora, and tell her that fhe did me injuftice.

Alonzo. *(Embracing him)* My friend, I have
words !—

Rolla. Do I not feel thy warm tears upon my ch
—Go, I am fully repaid.

Alonzo. In a few hours I return either to free th
to fhare thy death.

SCENE VII.—ROLLA *alone, looking after him.*

He is gone !—Now for the firft time in my life h
been guilty of deception !—the God of truth pardon
—He flatters himfelf with the hope of feeing me
fpeedily—Yes, in another world, perhaps—in a v
where Cora will love me !—Oh, felfifh man !—Is n
this done to ferve thyfelf, that when Cora fhall afcer
our common Father, her firft queftion may be, wh
Rolla ?—But, who comes here ?

SCENE VIII.—*Enter* ELVIRA.

Elvira. Well, Alonzo, have you confidered better of this matter? (*She perceives Rolla*) Ha! how is this? who art thou? where is Alonzo?

Rolla. Which queftion fhall I anfwer firft?

Elvira. Where is Alonzo?

Rolla. Gone.

Elvira. Efcaped?

Rolla. Yes.

Elvira. He muft be purfued. (*Going*)

Rolla. (*Stepping before her*) Hold!—that muft not be!

Elvira. Infolent man!—I will call the guards.

Rolla. Whatever you pleafe, fo that Alonzo gain time.

Elvira. (*Again endeavouring to go*) If you dare to touch me!—

Rolla. You ftir not from this place (*He clafps her in his arms*)

Elvira. (*Drawing a dagger*) This fhall force me a paffage;—through your heart.

Rolla. As you pleafe; but falling, I fhall ftill clafp you.

Elvira. Indeed!— Are fuch your fentiments?— The acquaintance of fuch a man is valuable. Releafe me;—I will rem in here.

Rolla. (*Quitting his hold*) It is enough!—Alonzo muft by this time be at fome diftance.

Elvira. And has efcaped by your help.

Rolla. By mine alone.

Elvira. How could you dare to run fo great a ha-zard?

Rolla. Why hefitate to encounter it?

Elvira. Are you prepared to fuffer death inftead of him?

Rolla. Should it be neceffary.

Elvira. You are no common friend.

Rolla. I am not actuated by friendship.

Elvira. By what motive then?

Rolla. 'Tis immaterial to you.

Elvira. I observe that you are sparing of your words.

Rolla. My province is rather to act, as you may perceive.

Elvira. Who are you?

Rolla. My name is Rolla.

Elvira. The Peruvian General?

Rolla. I was so, once.

Elvira. Is it possible?—you in our power?

Rolla. Perfectly so.

Elvira. You have been slighted, perhaps, and thirst of vengeance has driven you hither?

Rolla. What mean you by slighted?

Elvira. Your king has not rewarded you according to your deserts.

Rolla. Far beyond them.

Elvira. And yet you are here!—You are urged neither by thirst of revenge, nor by emotions of friendship— yet are here!

Rolla. Even so!

Elvira. I know of only one other passion which could prompt such rashness.

Rolla. And that is—

Elvira. Love.

Rolla. Right.

Elvira. You love then?—and whom?

Rolla. 'Tis immaterial to you.

Elvira. And you hope by this step—

Rolla. I do not hope any thing.

Elvira. I understand you now,—the object of your love is dead; and despair has brought you hither.

Rolla. As you please.

Elvira. I pity you sincerely.

Rolla. I thank you.

Elvira. Is your loss irreparable?

Rolla. Wholly irreparable.

Elvira. And at these early years, will you renounce life, and the enjoyment of your fame?

Rolla. Fame is only the gift of posterity.

Elvira.

Elvira. But fuppofing you could render farther fervices to your native country ?

Rolla. I fhall, unlefs put to death here.

Elvira. In what way ?

Rolla. By fighting againft you.

Elvira. And you dare to tell me that to my face ?

Rolla. 'Tis pity that you are not Pizarro.

Elvira. Why fo ?

Rolla, Then had I faid it to Pizarro's face.

Elvira. Ha !—you feem a man after my own heart.

Rolla. Refemble me then if you can.

Elvira. I refemble you!—I, a weak woman !

Rolla. A woman ?

Elvira, You are furprifed.

Rolla. No.

Elvira. True,—the hero fhould not be furprifed at any thing.

Rolla. Leaft of all at a woman.

Elvira. Not even if fhe were capable of a great action.

Rolla. Not even then.

Elvira. You refpect our fex ?

Rolla. It is better, and worfe, than ours.

Elvira. Suppofe I were to reftore you,—and with you the blefling of peace, to your native country ; would you reckon me among the better.

Rolla. Perhaps fo.

Elvira. Only *perhaps ?*

Rolla. Is it fufficient to fee the action, without knowing the motives that prompted it ?

Elvira. Proud man !—how is your friendfhip to be obtained ?

Rolla. By friendfhip.

Elvira. I will endeavour to obtain it. The morning but juft begins to dawn; there is yet time,—take this dagger and follow me.

Rolla. Whither ?

Elvira. I will conduct you to the tent, where Pizarro fleeps: you fhall difpatch him,—and then we will fly. Thus you will fave yourfelf from inevitable death, and deliver your native country from a dreadful fcourge.

Rolla. How has Pizarro injured you ?

Elvira. My love was firmly united to his fame. The fame

fame ftroke, which blafted the latter, has . annihilated the former.

Rolla. You loved him once ?

Elvira. So I thought, when I heard him the theme of univerfal admiration.

Rolla. And you now propofe that I fhould murder him in his fleep?

Elvira. Would he not have murdered Alonzo in chains ? We deal with him, only as he would deal with others. A man is equally defencelefs in chains, as when afleep.

Rolla. Give me the dagger.

Elvira. Take it.

Rolla. Now go on.

Elvira. You muft firft ftab the foldier who guards the tent.

Rolla. Muft I ?

Elvira. Elfe he will raife an alarm.

Rolla. Then, take back the dagger.

Elvira. Why fo ?

Rolla. This foldier is a man.

Elvira. Well ?

Rolla. A MAN !—Do you underftand me ?—Not every one who bears the human form deferves that name.

Elvira, What do you mean ?

Rolla, Againft gold this foldier was incorruptible. He was overcome by his feelings. He is my brother ; I will not injure him.

Elvira. Then we muft endeavour to deceive him.— Conceal the dagger.—What ho ! there ?—Guard !—

SCENE IX.—*The* SOLDIER *enters the Tent.*

Soldier. What would you have?

Elvira. Where is your prifoner ?

Soldier. Where, but here---(*He fees Rolla*) How !— What is the meaning of this ! (*He looks about*) Bleffed God ! Alonzo is gone !

Elvira. And you are loft.

Soldier.

Soldier. (*Addreſſing Rolla*) You have deceived me—Ah, I muſt die!—Oh my poor wife!—my poor children!

Rolla. Be not uneaſy—Pizarro has loſt nothing by the exchange—I pledge my word for your ſafety.

Elvira. And I mine. But the General muſt be immediately informed of the accident;—I will conduct this man to his tent.—Do you accompany us.

Soldier. He will order me to inſtant execution.

Elvira. Have we not both pledged ourſelves for his mercy?

Soldier. Ah, good lady!—for my poor children's ſake!—

Elvira. Only do as we deſire; and truſt to us, that not an hair of your head ſhall be touched. Come on, Rolla!—are you reſolved?

Rolla. I am ready to follow you.

Elvira. And may the angel appointed tod eſtroy tyrants, conduct our footſteps! [*Exeunt*

SCENE X.—*The inſide of* PIZARRO'S *tent.*

PIZARRO *alone, lying upon a couch; he toſſes about in diſturbed ſleep, and at intervals utters broken ſentences.*

Blood!—blood!—no mercy!—revenge!—revenge!—Off with his head!—there lies the trunk!—Ha! ha! ha! Look at the flaxen hair—all dyed with blood!—

SCENE XI.—*Enter* ROLLA *and* ELVIRA.

Elvira. There he lies—now, quickly!

Rolla. Go you, and leave me alone with him.

Elvira. Why ſo!

Rolla. I cannot ſtab in the preſence of a woman.

Elvira. But——

Rolla. Go, or I awaken him.

Elvira. Then, call me when the deed is done.

Rolla. Wait without.

Elvira.

Elvira. Be quick, left it be too late.   [*Exit*

Rolla. (*Goes up to Pizarro with folded arms, and obferves him earneftly*) And this is the man who has fo long
difturbed our peace ! the robber whom fome angry god has
fent as a fcourge among us !—He feems to be really afleep.
—Oh, God ! and can a Pizarro fleep !

Pizarro. Leave me !—leave me !—away ye phantoms !
—Oh !—oh !

Rolla. I was miftaken—he cannot fleep !—Come
hither, ye hardened villains !—look here !—fuch are the
flumbers of the wicked.

Pizarro. (*Starting up terrified*) Who's there !—Ho !
—Guards !

Rolla. (*Producing the dagger*) Not a word, or you die
this inftant.

Pizarro. Treafon ! treafon !

Rolla. Speak foftly, I command you!

Pizarro. And who are you?

Rolla. A Peruvian, as you fee, and my name is
Rolla. Your life is in my power,—to call for help would
be vain, for my arm would be quicker than your guard.

Pizarro. What would you have ?

Rolla. Not your life ; for had that been my aim, I
could have taken it as you flept ;—I forbore to do fo, be
not alarmed therefore for your fafety.

Pizarro. Speak, then, what is your bufinefs ?

SCENE XII.—*Re-enter* ELVIRA *haftily.*

Elvira. Ha ! how is this ! (*To Rolla*) Traitor !

Rolla. Rolla is no affaffin.

Pizarro. Who then is one ? (*He fixes his eyes on Elvira*) Thou !—thou '—bafe woman ?

Elvira. Had I loved affaffination, thy life had anfwered my purpofe better than thy death. But know,
that neither vengeance nor jealoufy urged me to this ftep—
humanity alone raifed my dagger againft thee. It was
aimed at the ravifher of crowns, the oppreffor of an injured
people. I wifhed to reftore to Peru that peace of which
                                                      thy

thy tyranny has deprived her; and 'twas therefore I refolved upon thy death.

Rolla. Had the deed been as noble as the end propofed, how had I admired you!

Elvira. The deed was noble, as the only means of at-
taining the nobleft objeƈt to which my heart ever afpired.
Oh, why did I not take the execution on myfelf!—why
did I entruft to another a work of fuch importance!—
Know, unfeafonable Philanthropift, that I had fhewn
more compaffion by ftriking this blow, than you have
fhewn by your forbearance!

Pizarro. Silence, frantic woman! and behold the compaffion I fhall extend to you! Ho, there!—Guards!
(Enter Guards) Seize this woman! fhe fought to murder your General. Let her be kept in the clofeft con-
finement, and let new torments be devifed—

Elvira. You remain PIZARRO, as I ELVIRA. Death
is to me a welcome friend, fince this ftroke has failed;—
yet, ere I go, hear me!—I would, through compaffion,
have difmiffed you from the world without torture; but
you are condemned by a fuperior power to breathe out
your foul amid the bittereft pangs of repentance, and the
fevereft lafhes of confcience.—Go on, then! murder me
alfo, thou fcourge of the human race! but remember that
thy deceitful tongue firft led me into the path of guilt—
firft beguiled me of my innocence, my happinefs! Do not
the laft words of my mother, as fhe curfed the feducer of
her child, ftill vibrate in thy ears?—Doft thou not hear
the groans of my dying brother, who, in feeking atone-
ment for a fifter's ruined honour, fell by thy murderous
fword?—Yes, tyrant!—tyrant!—whether thou fhalt follow me fooner or later into the gloomy fhades of death;
the fanfic which thou haft thyfelf prepared for thy reception, is ever ready to welcome thee!—the curfes of my
mother, the dying groans of my brother, and the fhrieks of
thoufands of innocent viƈtims, imprecating vengeance on
thy guilty head.

Pizarro. *(Endeavouring to fupprefs his agitation)* Will
no one fulfil my commands?

Elvira. You, Rolla, have deceived me; but accept
my forgivenefs: and let not your contempt follow me to
the grave. I was once innocent, pious, and a ftranger to
forrow. Oh! did you know the artifices by which this

L.   hypocrite

hypocrite deluded my guileless heart!—how he gradually undermined every virtuous principle in my bosom, and led me, step by step, into the abyss of vice, you must, you would. pity me!

Rolla. I pity you sincerely.

Elvira. Pity from thee is a cooling drop to assuage the fever that rages in my conscience.—Farewel!—*(To Pizarro)* And thou!—thou, who living, must anticipate the torments of a future world;—go on, pursue thy career of guilt, but remember, that the time will come when we shall meet again!—Yes, tyrant, we shall meet again!—The protracted torture with which I am threatened, I despise—my mind is still unconquered. —Greatly to live, has been denied me by fate!—It cannot prevent me from greatly dying!   [*Exeunt guards with Elvira.*

SCENE XIII.---Pizarro *and* Rolla.

Rolla. I would not, on any account, be in thy place!

Pizarro. Now, explain, I intreat, how this double miracle has been accomplished, that I should see thee here, and as the protector of my life.

Rolla. I came to rescue my friend, Alonzo.

Pizarro. Then art thou come in vain. My obligations to thee are great :---ask whatever thou wilt in acknowledgment of thy services, except the life of this man.

Rolla. He is no longer in thy power.

Pizarro. Who is no longer in my power?

Rolla. Alonzo.

Pizarro. He has escaped?

Rolla. Yes.

Pizarro. Curses on the boy!---how was that possible?

Rolla. How was it possible!---Thou despisest us as barbarians; but learn, that we are not strangers to the most powerful feelings of friendship.

Pizarro. Ha!---thou hast then dared——

Rolla. Disguised in the habit of a monk, I reached Alonzo's tent---made him assume my borrowed form,
                                                            under

under ſhelter of which he fled, while I rema'ned in his place.

Pizarro. Oh, you have deprived me of the nobleſt prize——

Rolla. He is a General, ſo am I. Take my life inſtead of his.

Pizarro. Peruvian, you extort my admiration.

Rolla. Yet I feel myſelf humbled, when I reflect that I muſt only ſhare this admiration with a woman. Elvira's viſit to him was, doubtleſs, with the ſame view.

Pizarro. Did Elvira viſit him ?---vile woman !---No, no, ſhe had far other motives,---ſhe meant to have confided to him the commiſſion, which, not finding him, ſhe entruſted to you. Oh ! then what gratitude ought I not to feel, that you promoted Alonzo's flight at ſo critical a moment !---had the dagger been placed in his hand inſtead of your's, my deſtruction had been inevitable.

Rolla. Think not ſo injuriouſly of my friend. He would have acted as I have done.

Pizarro. Of that I doubt; and muſt, therefore, continue to regard myſelf as deeply bound to you. Tell me how I can recompence a ſervice ſo important ?

Rolla. Can you make that a queſtion ?

Pizarro. You are at liberty.

Rolla. That I could not doubt.

Pizarro. Confeſs that thy enemy is not beneath thee in magnanimity.

Rolla. He does his duty.

Pizarro. Go, and ſhould we meet again with arms in our hands——

Rolla. We will fight as becomes men of valour.

Pizarro. I ſhall always avoid doing thee an injury.

Rolla. Do not ſay ſo; for, now I know thee, thou wilt be the firſt perſon I ſhall ſeek in the field or battle. Meanwhile, farewel !---God amend thee !---*(He is going, but returns)* Yet one word more. The ſoldier who guarded Alonzo's tent, performed his duty---he is innocent of the priſoner's eſcape---pardon him !

Pizarro. This is no ſlight requeſt.

Rolla. If it appear unreaſonable, let me remain here, and ſuffer whatever puniſhment he has incurred.

Pizarro. Would you hazard your life for a common ſoldier ?

Rolla.

Rolla. He is a man whom I have involved in misfortune.

Pizarro. Go in peace!---he has my pardon.

Rolla. Give me your hand upon it.

Pizarro. (Giving his hand) And let us be friends.

Rolla. Live quietly among us; serve your God peaceably. and leave us peaceably to serve ours; be the friend .of virtue, and you will be mine!

Pizarro. Consign over to me the object for which I contend,---the throne of Quito——

Rolla. Enough!---farewel!---   [*Exit.*

Pizarro. (Alone, after a pause) And I have suffered him to leave me quietly!---How dangerous it is to listen to the tongue of an enthusiast; since the mind is involuntarily swayed by his sentiments.---But I have given him my word.---My word!---And must I now consult the chaplain, to ascertain how far I am bound to keep my faith with a heathen?---But this heathen is a hero, and heroes throughout the world are of the same creed.---
[*Exit.*

SCENE XIV.---*An open place near the Peruvian camp.*
ATALIBA *reposing under a tree.*

How silent and desolate seems every thing around! ---Are not our feelings much the same after a victory, as after a fever? while we would fain rejoice over the danger past, there is scarcely strength remaining to utter our joy ---our smiles are drowned by tears, and the acclamations we hear are only echoed by a sigh. What a dearly-earned prize is victory!---The records of history, while they tell of the numbers that fall in battle, are silent as to those whom every conflict renders miserable.--The barbed arrow appears to strike only one heart, but in that one, it often pierces an hundred. Oh, how gladly would I exchange all my victories for a single harvest-home!

SCENE

SCENE XV.---*Enter a* COURTIER.

Courtier. The herald is returned, but brings us no confolation.

Ataliba. Is Alonzo dead?

Courtier. He is ftill alive, but the Spaniards rejeát the proffered ranfom. " Your treafures," they arrogantly fay, " are ours ; within a few days they will be in our " poffeffion, and we fhall be your lords. In our power, " confifts our right."

Ataliba. Not yet humbled. Are frefh fupplies continually rifing up among thefe ferpents that hifs around my throne?---Where is Alonzo's wife?

Courtier. Fled with her child,---but no one knows whither.---Rolla too has difappeared.---The army ftands in mute aftonifhment at the tidings.

Ataliba. Rolla gone!---impoffible!---Rolla forfake me! when I am furrounded by diftrefs and danger!---Oh, God! is there no one to relieve the cares of royalty?--- how gladly would I exchange fituations with the lowett among my fubjects!

SCENE XVI.---*Enter* ALONZO *in his difguife.*

Alonzo. Do I behold my fovereign once more?

Ataliba. Alonzo!---Art thou, indeed, Alonzo?

Alonzo. Where is my wife?

Ataliba. Oh welcome, but unexpeéted fight!

Alonzo. Where is my wife?

Ataliba. How did you efcape?

Alonzo. Almoft by a miracle.

Ataliba. Say how?

Alonzo. Who but Rolla could have made fuch a facrifice to the facred glow of friendfhip?---Who but Rolla could have forced his way to my prifon, under fuch a difguife?---He it was who loofened my chains to fix them upon himfelf.

Ataliba.

Ataliba. Rolla in the enemy's power!---Ah! thou haft indeed wounded me afrefh.

Alonzo. Give me a fword, with five hundred refolute men, that I may haften to fave him!

Ataliba. Shall I hazard in you my laft fupport?

Alonzo. The enemy is difpirited; the camp on the right fide weakly fortified; Pizarro has made himfelf odious by his barbarities; the foldiers begin to murmur againft him; let us not leave them time to recollect themfelves. One more victory, and we fhall drive them back to the ocean, where the waves will fwallow up our plagues, and their rapacity.

Ataliba. Well then, I will myfelf furvey their camp, to afcertain where, and how, an attack may be poffible.

Alonzo. Oh, do not expofe yourfelf to fuch danger!--- Conlider that you are our king.

Ataliba. Wherever danger may threaten the children, thither the father fhould haften himfelf.

Alonzo. No, leave it to me!---only fuffer me firft to embrace my deareft wife.

Ataliba. (With embarraffment) Your wife?

Alonzo. Cora muft, undoubtedly, have fuffered much upon my account.

Ataliba. Alas! fhe has fuffered moft feverely!

Alonzo. But in another moment her fufferings fhall be at an end.

Ataliba. Where would you feek her?

Alonzo. Is fhe not here?

Ataliba. Anguifh has driven her hence.

Alonzo. Whither?

Ataliba. Alas! we know not. Perhaps among the mountains, to her father.

Alonzo. Oh, God! what a fhivering has feized my whole frame.

Courtier. She was feen upon the field of battle, and heard to call upon your name till night came on, when fhe rufh.d into the foreft.

Alonzo. Into the foreft!---which fwarms with the ene-my!-- *(Going)*

Ataliba. Alonzo, whither would you go?

Alonzo. Whitherfoever defpair and anguifh may drive me!---Good Inca, thou art fafe; the vanquifhed enemy dare not at prefent hazard an attack. Oh then, thou pro-

                                    tector

tector of every right! respect the rights of nature ; my
Cora, my child, my all, is loft!---Releafe the General
for a few moments from his duty, that the hufband may
feek his diftracted wife.

Ataliba. I participate in your agony!---Go, but do
not forget Rolla.

Alonzo. Cora!---Rolla!---Some good angel direct my
uncertain fteps!---   [*Exit.*

Ataliba. (*To the Courtier*) Lend me your fword for a
moment. (*The Courier gives him his fword; the King endeavours to brandifh it, but finds himfelf unable*). It will
not do!---Unhappy king!---What avail a prudent head
and a willing heart, when the ftrength is wholly exhaufted!---   [*Exeunt.*

END OF THE FOURTH ACT.

ACT V.

SCENE I.---*A thick Forest. In the Back Ground a Hut formed of Boughs of Trees. Thunder and Lightning.*

CORA *enters with her Child in her Arms; her Hair hangs wildly about her Neck; she pants for Breath, and appears nearly exhausted.*

CORA.

I CAN no more!---Nature is weaker than Love!—my heart would urge me forwards---but---my strength is gone! ---Sweet child! how soundly he sleeps!---Ah! his father sleeps too!---The child will wake again; but the father, never!---never!---Oh! why am I a mother?---why does this infant chain me to life?---Miserable wretch that I am; I dare not die!---Where am I?---Whither does anguish drive me?---The lightning flashes among the trees, but it shews no path--- The thunder rolls among the mountains, and overpowers my feeble voice---I can go no further---my feet will no longer bear me. (*She sinks down under a tree.*) Still dost thou sleep, smiling angel?--Glare around, ye lightnings! Roll on, thou thunder! yet this infant innocence still slumbers securely in his mother's arms. I will make a bed of mofs and leaves, and spread my veil over him,---then lie down by his side and die. (*She collects mofs and leaves, and makes a bed for her child, then lays him down, and covers him with her veil.*) There lie and sleep; and mayst thou never awake to feek in vain for nourishment at the breast of thy lifeless mother!--- A mift obscures my senses!---every limb is faint; every nerve unstrung!---Is this death? (*She leans against a tree.*)

(*Alonzo's*

(*Alonzo's voice is heard at a diſtance*) Cora!

Cora. (*Starting*) What ſound was that?

Alonzo. (*Still at a diſtance*) Cora!

Cora. Is it the echo of the thunder among the mountains?

Alonzo. Cora!

Cora. Hark!—did'n't I hear a ſpirit call!

Alonzo. (*Somewhat nearer*) Cora!

Cora. Oh, my heart, do not deceive me!—It is
Alonzo's voice!

Alonzo. (*Still ſomewhat nearer*) Cora!

Cora. (*Moving a few ſteps towards the voice*) Alonzo,
where are you?

Alonzo. Cora!

Cora. (*Following the voice a few ſteps further*) 'Tis
he! Alonzo!

Alonzo. (*Approaching*) Cora!

Cora. (*Still going towards the ſound*) I ſeem to gain
new ſtrength.—Alonzo!

Alonzo. Cora! where are you?

Cora. Here!—here!— (*She diſappears among the trees;
her voice and Alonzo's are heard for ſome time, calling to each
other,—till at laſt by a reciprocal exclamation of tranſport,
they appear to have met.*)

SCENE II.—*Enter two* SPANISH SOLDIERS, *drunk.*

Firſt Soldier. Brother, whither are you leading me?

Second. Wherever you pleaſe, brother.

Firſt. We have loſt our way.

Second. We ſhall do, if we keep the Sun on our left
hand.

Firſt. The Sun!---Can you ſee the ſun?

Second. Fool! who can ſee the ſun when 'tis behind thunder-clouds?

Firſt. Then, if we keep the lightning on the left
hand?---

Second. That will do as well.—We are not far from
the camp; I heard the outpoſt's call. Co

Firſt. That's the watch-word, I ſuppoſe.

Second. Aye, aye, come along. (*They perceive the
child.*)

M   *Firſt.*

Firſt. Halloo! brother! What have we here?

Second. A child, as I live!

Firſt. How came it here?

Second. What is to be done with it?

Firſt. 'Tis no concern of ours; let it lie; 'tis a hea-then's child.

Second. It ſleeps ſo ſweetly.---I have one at home, juſt like it.----I have a great mind to take it with me.

Firſt. Take it, if you pleaſe; but don't give it to me if you find it heavy, and grow tired of it.

Second. (Taking the child in his arms) Poor little duer! 'tis as light as a feather.

Firſt. 'Tis plaguy dark, here :---out of the foreſt, we ſhall have more light.

Second. Well, well, go on!

[*Exeunt ſoldiers with the child.*

Cora's voice is heard on the oppoſite ſide. This way, Alonzo, it was here I left him.

Second Soldier. (Behind the ſcenes) The boughs run into one's eyes, at every ſtep.

Cora. (Approaching nearer) My heart cannot deceive me; I am ſure we are at the ſpot.

Soldier (At a greater diſtance) Down yonder to the left, I ſee the camp.

SCENE III.   *Enter* CORA *and* ALONZO.

Cora. Here is the place; it was under this tree!—
(She runs up to the tree, but finding only the veil, and the child gone, ſhe ſhrieks, and ſinks to the ground.)

Alonzo (Throwing himſelf by her) Cora, what is the matter?

Cora (Raiſing herſelf up) He is gone!

Alonzo. Eternal God!

Cora. He is gone!

Alonzo. Let us ſeek him.

Cora. My child!—O my child!

Alonzo. Where did he lie?

Cora. (Throwing herſelf on the ſpot) Here!

Alonzo.

Alonzo. He waked, and has crawled to a little diftance.

Cora. (*Starts up and searches about*) Oh, no!---he is
gone!

Alonzo. Be calm; he will certainly be found.

Cora. Fernando!---my Fernando!

Alonzo. He cannot be far off. Are you certain this
was the place?

Cora. Was not the veil lying here?---He is torn in
pieces by wild beasts!

Alonzo. Do not think the worst.

Cora. I cannot think---I only see my mangled
child.

Alonzo. Cora, for God's fake---

Cora. There is no God!

Alonzo. What a dreadful affertion!

Cora. What have I done to deferve the load of mifery
heaped upon me?

Alonzo. Cora!---deareft wife!---calm thefe tranfports!

Cora. (*Lifting her eyes to heaven*) Give me my child,
or death!

Alonzo. Do you not fee a hut among the trees?

Cora. Ha!---there lives the wretch who has robbed
me of my child! (*She haftens towards the hut*)

Alonzo. Cora, beware; it may be inhabited by Spaniards.

Cora. I will go, were it the abode of dæmons!

Alonzo. Let me go firft. (*Knocks at the door*)

SCENE IV. *Enter* LAS-CASAS, *from the Hut.*

Las-Cafas. Who knocks?

Cora. Give me back my child.

Las-Cafas. Young woman, what would you have?

Alonzo. Oh, God! do not my eyes deceive me!---
Las-Cafas?

Las-Cafas. Alonzo, do I behold thee again? (*Embracing him*)

Alonzo. My kind inftructor!

Las-Cafas. My beloved friend!

M 2 *Cora*

Cora. Where have you concealed my child?

Las-Cafas. What is the meaning of this?

Alonzo. In what a moment of diftrefs, have we met again!

Cora. Good. old man, you feem not deftitute of humanity,—have compaffion upon a wretched mother!

Las-Cafas. I do not underftand you.

Cora. I will be your fervant as long as I live;—my child fhall be your flave.

Las-Cafas. Is fhe diftracted?

Alonzo. She is my wife; we have loft our child.

Las-Cafas. Where did you lofe him?

Alonzo. He was left fleeping under yon' tree.

Las-Cafas. Did you leave him?

Cora. Oh, you are right! I was an unnatural mother; I forfook my child; the chaftifement of the gods purfues me.

Las-Cafas. Would that it were in my power to afford you confolation!

Alonzo. Affift me to fupport this mifery.

Cora. (*Diftracted*) Look at the fpeckled fnake; how he winds round the child's body!---Ha! hear how the venomous reptile hiffes---fee! with his fting he pierces my poor boy's heart!

Alonzo. Deareft Cora, recollect yourfelf.

Cora. Look at the dreadful Condor, hovering in the air!---See! he darts down upon his prey; he fixes his claws in the helplefs creature!---Ha! look at the favage Tyger, crouching behind the bufh---fee! he fprings forward---look! the blood gufhes out! help! help! (*She throws herfelf upon the ground*)

Alonzo. (*Kneeling by her*) Oh, my wife!---my fon!---

Las-Cafas. And, muft the form of mifery purfue me, even into this defert?

Alonzo. Confole us, Las-Cafas! — my kind inftructor, confole us! do not forfake us at this dreadful hour!

Las-Cafas. I will remain with you; but we are not fafe near the Spanifh camp. Haften to your own friends; I will accompany you.

Alonzo. How fhall we bear away this poor creature?

Las-Cafas. Let us endeavour to recover her.

Alonzo. Come, deareft Cora, let us go.

Cora.

Cora. (*Raifing her head*) Go!—whither ?

Alonzo. To our own camp.

Cora. Shall I leave this fpot ?—this fpot where my child died !

Alonzo. We are fo near the enemy.

Cora. Barbarian !—will you even prevent my collect-ing the bones of my child.

Alonzo. Thy father and brother are arrived at the camp.

Cora. I have neither father nor brother.—I once had a fon.

Alonzo. We will feek for him.

Cora. (*Springing up*) Seek for him ! Oh, where ! where !

Alonzo. And this old man will affift us.

Cora. Yes, good old man, affift us to look for him !

Las-Cafas. Moft willingly ; only be calm.

Cora. Have you any children ?

Las-Cafas. No.

Cora. Then I can pardon you. Would you calm a mother, give her back her loft child. (*She rufhes out*)

Las-Cafas. (*Haftening after her*) Endeavour to lead her to the right ;—that way lies your camp.

Alonzo. The fight of you was to me like beholding an angel. [*Exeunt.*

SCENE V.—*An out-poft of the Spanifh camp.*

ROLLA *bound in chains, is dragged in by feveral foldiers.*

A Soldier. Hither, thou worfhipper of idols.

Rolla. I was fet at liberty by Pizarro himfelf.

Soldier. We know nothing about that, and no heathen efcapes from us with life,—much lefs with liberty. Come, away to the General's tent.

Another Soldier. Silence, brother !—behold the General.

Pizarro. (*Entering*) What is the matter here ?—Ha ! —Do I fee right ?—Rolla ?

Rolla. (*Sarcaftically*) Yes, Rolla !—To your aftonifh-ment, I fuppofe.

Pizarro

Pizarro. And bound !

Rolla. So faſt that he need not give you any uneasineſs.

Pizarro. Who has dared to treat thus injuriouſly the man that ſaved my life.

Soldier. He acknowledges himſelf to be a General among his own people. He wanted to ſteal through our outpoſts.

Rolla. (*Contemptuouſly*) Steal !

Soldier. We ſtopped him ; and Almagro ordered us to put him in chains.

Pizarro. (*To Rolla*) You find that I am innocent of this. (*To the Soldiers*) Take off his chains ! (*They obey*) It is humiliating, to behold a hero like Rolla unarmed ; take this. (*Gives him a ſword*) Now, underſtand the Spaniſh character. We can eſteem generoſity even in an enemy.

Rolla. (*Taking the Sword*) And a Peruvian knows how to forget injuries. I pardon you.

Pizarro. Nor will you, I truſt, withdraw that pardon, even though I ſhould confeſs, that I cannot be angry with my people, ſince I am indebted to this accident for a ſecond interview with ſuch a man.

Rolla. Enough of ſmooth words—let me depart.

Pizarro. At your own pleaſure. Yet ſuffer me to cheriſh the pleaſing hope, that this renewed acquaintance may be the means of bringing us to a better underſtanding. Rolla and Pizarro were not created to live in eternal enmity.

Rolla. I promiſe thee my friendſhip, as ſoon as the ocean ſhall lie between us.

Pizarro. How, if we could be united by one common object ?—When we met before, you heard with impatience my hopes of aſcending the throne of Quito. That idea I now renounce, and only aſk that you ſubmit to the Spaniſh ſceptre, and embrace the Chriſtian faith ; then will peace be eſtabliſhed between us on a ſolid and permanent baſis.

Rolla. Wonderful moderation !

Pizarro. On Pizarro's friendſhip hangs the protection of a mighty monarch ; and this friendſhip Pizarro offers, while he tenders you his hand.

Rolla.

Rolla. Rolla is no traitor.

Pizarro. By accepting the offer, you will avert a load of misery from your country.

Rolla. I owe my country, the sacrifice of my life, but not of my honour.

Pizarro. You would only deprive a weak king of a station to which he is unequal.

Rolla. Ataliba weak!--- But were he so, a king who makes his people happy, is strong in his people's love.

Pizarro. Confider this propofal well.

Rolla. It has been long decided by my confcience.

Pizarro. Recollect, that defpifed friendfhip, rages with no lefs fury than defpifed love.

Rolla. Ha!---this is what I expected!---Why thus torment thyfelf, to feek for flimfy fubterfuges ?---Throw off the mafk at once.

Pizarro. (*Endeavouring to fmother his rage*) Rolla, do not miftake me!

Rolla. May I depart?

Pizarro. (*After a ftruggle*) Yes, --you may depart.

Rolla. Will nothing obftruct my return to our own camp?

Pizarro. Nothing --- unlefs repentance bring you back to us.

Rolla. Thanks to the gods! Rolla never found caufe to repent any action of his life!

SCENE VI. --- *Enter the two* SOLDIERS *with the* CHILD.

Firft Soldier. General, we have found a child.

Pizarro. What is that to me?---away with you.

Soldier. It was lying in the foreft, not far from the camp.

Pizarro. Throw it into the firft ditch you find.

Rolla.

Rolla. Gracious God! it is Alonzo's child.

Pizarro. How!

Rolla. (*To the Soldiers*) Give it to me.

Pizarro (*Stepping in between them*) Not fo hafty!—— Alonzo's child---did you fay?---Fortunate chance!--- welcome, little creature!--- thou fhalt ferve me as a fcourge to chaftife thy father's follies.

Rolla. Does Pizarro make war on children?

Pizarro. You cannot underftand me. I have an old account to fettle with Alonzo. I might inftantly pay my debt by plunging a dagger into the breaft of this child; but that were merely to *pay* him,—and I muft now make him *my* debtor.

Rolla. You are right—I do not underftand you.

Pizarro. What think you of elevating this little head upon the point of a lance?—Then, when the hero, Alonzo, fhall be preffing forward through the thickeft ranks of the enemy, bearing down all before him, like the waters of a rufhing ftream; what will be the mound to ftop his pro-grefs?—the head of a child. See, where the hero ftands motionlefs as a ftatue;—his fword falls from his palfied hand;—his eyes are immovably fixed, with a ftare of horror, upon the bloody banner, from which drops ftill trickle down upon the lance.—This will be a fight!' (*With malicious exultation.*)

Rolla. Pizarro, are you a man!

Pizarro. And when he returns home to the eagerly-expecting mother, as fhe throws her fnowy arms around his neck, and with her filken hair wipes the bloody drops from his fhoulder; then will he fay, with a tender kifs, " My love! you fuppofe this to be the blood of an " enemy—but no, no, it flowed from the veins of thine " own child!"—Oh, glorious—

Rolla. Look, how the infant fmiles!—And could you murder fuch innocence?

Pizarro. Could you wring the neck of a dove?

Rolla. Do you want a ranfom?—I will fend you ten times the boy's weight in filver.

Pizarro. Let it be caft into a ftatue of him, and placed upon his grave.

Rolla.

Rolla. Pizarro, you thanked me for your life; give me in return, the life of this child.

Pizarro. Do you seek to shame me by so paltry a request?

Rolla. Send back the child, and I will remain your prisoner.

Pizarro. You are at full liberty.

Rolla. Surely it is impossible that nature can have put thee out of her hands, in a manner so careless and unfinished, as not to have given human feelings to thy heart.—Behold me at thy feet,—the man who saved thy life,—who devotes himself to be thy slave, if thou will surrender this child to his parents!

Pizarro. The child shall remain here.

Rolla. (*With growing rage*) Pizarro hear me!

Pizarro. Either you instantly become the vassals of Spain, or this child remains my prisoner.

Rolla. Well then!—(*He springs forwards, hastily snatches the child from the soldier, clasps it with his left arm, and with his right draws his sword*) I have not received this weapon in vain,—this child is mine;——who dares attempt to follow me, dies. (*Exit hastily*)

Pizarro. Fool-hardy boaster!—audacious madman!—away soldiers, hasten after him; and, if possible, bring him back alive. (*Exeunt several soldiers*) What dæmon possesses this man!——Fool that I was, to give him a sword! (*Looking after Rolla*) How the madman defends himself!—he gains ground of his pursuers——by Heaven he will escape them!—away, more of you join the pursuit; no longer attempt to preserve his life—(*Exeunt other Soldiers*) Ah! I can no longer see him; the hill now conceals him from me. Madman, do not impute thy death to me!—I would gladly have made thee my friend, and discharged the obligations I owe thee. (*Several guns are heard fired at a distance*) Farewel!—thou hast deserved an honourable death! (*Enter a Soldier*)—Well, what news?

Soldier. Be satisfied, General, the hero cannot proceed much farther; a shot hit him on the right side, and I saw him fall.

Pizarro. More gladly would I have heard that he was

N   taken

taken alive. Prefumptuous heathen !—to offer me defiance, in my own camp.

Soldier. Your order to fpare him, has coft the lives of four of our foldiers. (*Another Soldier enters*)

Second Soldier. He has forced his way through every obftacle, and reached the out-pofts of his own camp.

Pizarro. (*Stamping upon the ground*) Curfed fortune !

Second Soldier. But he is mortally wounded,—His death is certain.

Pizarro. And notwithftanding that, forced his way through ?

Soldier. Never did I behold courage equal to his. All the fabulous feats of our Moorifh knights, are nothing, compared with what he has actually performed. Four of us, who endeavoured to take him alive, fell by his fword. A fhot from another levelled him with the ground ; but he inftantly ftarted up again, laid the child down, and leaning againft a tree, dealt his ftrokes round him every way, like the angel with the flaming fword, till two more were ftretched dead at his feet. The reft then began to prepare their fire-arms, when he caught up the child, and darting forwards like an arrow, was quickly out of their reach— but the tree againft which he had leaned, and the place where he ftood, were dyed with blood ; and by his blood, every ftep that he ran might be traced. The foldiers fired feveral fhot after him, but he foon difappeared behind the hill.

Pizarro. Why did you not mount your horfes ?

Soldier. They were grazing behind the camp.

Pizarro. Curfed idoltater !—and yet I cannot refufe him my warmeft admiration. Give me a thoufand fuch men,—and I would conquer the world. (*Exeunt.*)

SCENE VII.—*An open place near the Peruvian camp.*

ATALIBA *enters with folded arms, and wrapped in thought.*

The enemy is quiet, my army fleeps, the ftorm has paffed over, and no breath of wind whifpers among the trees.—A

deep

deep and folemn filence reigns around, and all things both in the animate and the inanimate creation, feem to tafte repofe,—all but my throbbing heart. Why is that ftill reftlef ? Why muft I alone be haunted by the phantoms of the flain ? Why muft I alone be inceffantly tormented with ideal founds, as of dying groans ?—Was is not for God and my native land, that my fword was drawn?

SCENE VIII.—*Enter* CORA *diftracted.*

Cora. Whither do you lead me ?—Where is my child's grave ? *(Seeing Ataliba.)* Ha!—thou firft-born of the Sun, give me back my child.

Ataliba. Cora, whence come you ?

Cora. From the grave where they have laid my child. Oh! it is deep in the earth!—there all is cold and damp— Oh—h—h! how I fhiver!

Ataliba. Ah! fight of woe! *(Enter Alonzo and Las-Cafas)*

Alonzo. Unhappy creature! whither does thy mifery lead thee?

Cora. Silence! Alonzo, behold here, the firft-born of our God!—the Sun is his father; he has only to fpeak the word,—and the grave will give back its prey. *(She clafps Ataliba's knees)* Speak, my king!—have compaffion upon a mother's anguifh!

Ataliba. Oh, God! what does fhe mean ?

Alonzo. We have loft our child.

Ataliba. Wretched mother!—alas, I cannot help thee; —I am only a king.

Cora. To whom, then, am I to apply?—to whom, but thee, have the gods entrufted our lives?—Was it not by thee that the Peruvians were led to battle?—Did not my Alonzo fight for thee?—wilt thou refufe the only recom-pence we afk for all that he has done,—the life of a child who fhall himfelf one day take arms for thy defence.

Ataliba. Crufh me, ye gods! I will meet my fate with refignation!

Cora. *(Springing up)* Oh, tyrant!—canft thou witnefs

N 2   my

my anguish, unmoved?—Is not thy ambition yet satiated
with blood?——Is it not enough, that, to every one
of these diamonds hangs a drop of the vital stream?—
but must thou also tear children from their mother's breasts,
and cast them to the wild beasts?—Ha! what is the dia-
dem to me? what to me the throne of Quito?—hither,
hither, ye mothers, whom this victory has made childless!
hither to me! help me to curse! that our misery may ascend
to heaven with the exultations of this barbarian!—And, if
hereafter he shall experience the anguish of only one wretched mother; he will be sufficiently tormented! (*She sinks
exhausted upon the ground*)

Alonzo. (*To Ataliba, as he catches Cora in his arms*) Forgive a mother's distraction!

Ataliba. (*Wiping tears from his eyes*) The throne
has no charms which can atone for witnessing such
agony.

Cora. (*Smiling*) Alonzo bring me the child, that he
may receive his accustomed nourishment. Inhuman, Alonzo! you see me dying, yet will not let me feast once more
upon his infant smiles!

Alonzo. This complaining is more painful than even
thy rage. Yes, unhappy mother! rage on, thou hast no
longer a child!

Cora. (*Falling back*) Unhappy mother! thou hast no
longer a child!

SCENE IX.—*Enter a* PERUVIAN

Peruvian. Rolla is hastening hither.

Ataliba and Alonzo. Rolla! (*Rolla staggers upon the
stage, with a death like paleness in his countenance, the bloody
sword in his right hand, and the child in his left*)

Ataliba. Oh God! what do I see!

Rolla. (*In a faint voice, and sinking upon his knee, unable to approach the fainting Cora*) Cora!—your child!

Cora. (*Opening her eyes, and seeing the child, starts up
and stretches out her arms to receive him*) My child!—
and covered with blood.

Rolla. (*Holding out the child to her*) It is my blood.

Cora.

Cora. (*Clasping the child to her breast*) My child!
Oh Rolla!

Rolla. I loved thee!—thou haft fufpected me unjuftly!
I can no more! (*He finks down*)

Alonzo. (*Throwing himfelf by him*) Rolla! thou dieft!

Rolla. For Cora. (*Expires*)

Cora. (*Looking with agony at the body*) Did ever man
love like this man?—Oh child too dearly purchafed!

Alonzo. Las-Cafas, help me to believe in a juft God!

Las-Cafas. His ways are incomprehenfible!—pray to
him, and be refigned!

(*The Curtain falls.*)

END OF THE PLAY.

www.ingramcontent.com/pod-product-compliance
Lightning Source LLC
Chambersburg PA
CBHW032156010726
47493CB00008BA/2718